HARPER LEE'S

To Kill a Mockingbird

Dramatized by
CHRISTOPHER SERGEL

Dramatic Publishing
Woodstock, Illinois • London, England • Melbourne, Australia

*** NOTICE ***

TO KILL A MOCKINGBIRD
A Full-Length Play
For Twelve Men* and Eight Women, Extras

CHARACTERS

JEAN LOUISE FINCH . . . . Scout as a grown-up woman

SCOUT . . . . a young girl

JEM . . . . her brother

ATTICUS . . . . their father

CALPURNIA . . . . the housekeeper

MAUDIE ATKINSON

STEPHANIE CRAWFORD

MRS. DUBOSE . . . . neighbors

NATHAN RADLEY

ARTHUR RADLEY (BOO)

DILL . . . . a young boy

HECK TATE . . . . the sheriff

JUDGE TAYLOR . . . . the judge

REVEREND SYKES . . . . a minister

MAYELLA EWELL . . . . a young woman

BOB EWELL . . . . her father

WALTER CUNNINGHAM . . . . a farmer

MR. GILMER . . . . public prosecutor

TOM ROBINSON . . . . a young man

HELEN ROBINSON . . . . his wife

TOWNSPEOPLE

FARMERS

PLACE: Maycomb, Alabama

TIME: 1935

*Boo Radley and Nathan Radley may be played by the same actor.

SETTING

There may be a curtain, but it isn't necessary. The set which stands throughout the play can be visible to the audience as they take their seats in the theatre.

The intention of the set is to suggest a part of a house and the immediate neighborhood just outside, in a small town in the southern part of Alabama. It is 1935, and while the set need not reflect this in detail, a few props that suggest the period (available, no doubt, from someone's attic) are recommended.

The stage has two levels. At the right on the lower level is the porch of the Finch home. It has several old rockers, chairs, possibly an old-fashioned radio and a porch swing or glider.

On the upper level, suggesting the street, are several narrow porch fronts with doorways behind. The porches have railings, and if desired, there may be flowers or shrubs about them. The Dubose porch, ULC, should have at least a few potted flowers. The actors must have access to these porches from behind, and there should be a passageway in front of the porches, but still on the platform, on which an actor can cross the stage from right to left. This passageway also makes room for an inner curtain that can be drawn across (or lowered) in front of the upper level porches.

At the left side of the stage is a part of another house. It's a slate-gray house with dark green shutters beside a window with heavy curtains behind. There is a closed door and a picket fence. The place is neglected, and to a child, it could seem ominous. It is on the upper level, though the little section of picket fence is in front of it on the lower level. Just outside the fence and at the left is a tree.

ACT ONE

THE HOUSELIGHTS DIM and in the darkness there are the soft sounds of birds, and in the distance, a dog barking.

The stage light comes up, revealing a girl who is now sitting in the porch swing (or glider) thoughtfully swinging back and forth. Her hair is plain and she wears bib overalls.

A woman, dressed in simple modern clothes, comes on the lower level, L. If possible, there should be something about her that suggests the girl-in-the-swing, grown older, for this is who she is. The woman, Jean Louise Finch, was called "Scout" when she was young, and so the young girl in the swing will be called SCOUT, while the same person, grown older, is called JEAN.

JEAN is looking about as though seeing this place in memory. As she comes up to the tree, she reaches up and touches a place on the trunk.

JEAN (smiling as she speaks; softly and to herself). The cement would still be there covering the knothole. (A voice is heard calling from off R. It's the voice of CALPURNIA.)

CALPURNIA (calling). Scout -- where are you? Scout, you come here.

JEAN. My name is Jean Louise, but when I was that young girl there on the swing . . . they called me "Scout. "

CALPURNIA. You hear me, Scout?

SCOUT (still swinging; preoccupied). I'm watching for Atticus.

JEAN. Atticus -- that's my father. Back then he seemed ancient . . . feeble.

He was a lawyer and nearly fifty. When my brother Jem asked him why he was so old, he said he got started late -- which we thought reflected on his manliness. He was much older than the parents of our school contemporaries and there was nothing Jem or I could say about him.

SCOUT (speaking forward). Because he doesn't do anything. Atticus doesn't drive a dump truck for the county, he isn't sheriff, he doesn't farm, or work in a garage, or anything worth mentioning. Other fathers go hunting, play poker, or fish. Atticus works in an office, and he reads.

JEAN. With those attributes, however, Atticus did not remain as inconspicuous as Jem and I might have wished. (With feeling.) No, he did not!

BOY'S VOICE (calling from off L). Hey, Scout -- how come your daddy defends niggers? (Singsong.) Scout's daddy defends nig . . . gers! (SCOUT has risen and come to the porch railing, her fists clenched.)

SCOUT. You gonna take that back, boy?

BOY'S VOICE. You gonna make me? My folks say your daddy's a disgrace and that nigger oughta hang from the water tank.

SCOUT. You take that back!

BOY'S VOICE (going away). Make me! Try and make me!

CALPURNIA (voice offstage R). Scout. I've told you to come in.

SCOUT. I' m not ready to come in. (Going back to swing.) I have to talk to Atticus.

JEAN. It was Maycomb, Alabama and it was back in 1935 when I was that girl -- back when ugly words were first shouted at us -- back at the beginning of an experience that brought a man to his death. (Looks toward house L.) And it brought Boo Radley storming out of that shutup house -- the attack on me -- Jem's arm broken -- another man killed! (Turning back front.) But that isn't what I want to remember. That's not why my mind's come back here. (Trying to sort this out.) There's something I have to do -- something my father wanted. Probably enough years have gone by -- enough so I can look back -- perhaps even enough so now I can do the one thing my father asked. (Correcting herself with a smile. Almost an afterthought.) No -- there was one other thing. When he gave us air rifles, he asked us never to kill a mockingbird.

(MISS MAUDIE ATKINSON has come out on her porch.)

MISS MAUDIE (to JEAN LOUISE). Your father's right. Mockingbirds just make music. They don't eat up people's gardens, don't nest in corncribs; they don't do one thing but sing their hearts out. That's why it's a sin to kill a mockingbird.

SCOUT (crossing to porch rail). Miss Maudie -- this is an old neighborhood, ain't it?

MISS MAUDIE (turning toward SCOUT). Been here longer than the town.

SCOUT. No, I mean the folks on our street are all old. Jem and me's the only children. Mrs. Dubose is close on a hundred and Miss Crawford's old and so are you and Atticus.

MISS MAUDIE (tartly). Not being wheeled around yet. Neither's your father. You're lucky. You and Jem have the benefit of your father's age. If your father was thirty, you'd find life quite different.

SCOUT (emphatically). I sure would. Atticus can't do anything.

MISS MAUDIE. You'd be surprised. There's life in him yet.

SCOUT. What can he do?

MISS MAUDIE. Quite a lot. (Going.) Seems to me you'd be proud of him.

SCOUT (calling after her; concerned). Why? The way some folks are starting to go on, you'd think he was running a still. (Realizing Miss Maudie is gone, she returns to swing.) I have to speak to him.

JEAN (crossing). We lived over there -- Atticus, my brother Jem, and Calpurnia, our cook -- who raised us. Calpurnia was all angles and bones.

(CALPURNIA has come out on the porch.)

CALPURNIA. You come in and wash up before your father gets home.

SCOUT (rising, but under protest). I said I wasn't ready.

CALPURNIA. Your brother's already washed. Why don't you behave as well as Jem?

SCOUT. Because he's older than me and you know it.

CALPURNIA (giving her a swat to encourage her along). Get in there.

(They are both going into the house.)

JEAN. Calpurnia's hand was as hard as a bed slat. My mother died when I was two, so I never felt her absence. (Smiles wryly.) But I felt Calpurnia's tyrannical presence as long as I could remember.

SCOUT (voice, from inside house). The water's too hot.

CALPURNIA (voice, also inside house; unimpressed). Keep scrubbin'!

JEAN (considering neighborhood). Even in 1935, Maycomb, Alabama was already a tired old town.

(HECK TATE and JUDGE TAYLOR enter on the upper level L, and are crossing R.)

JEAN (continuing). In rainy weather the streets turned to red slop; grass grew on the sidewalks, the courthouse sagged in the square. (Noticing.) That's Heck Tate -- the sheriff, and Judge Taylor.

HECK (calling). Atticus -- you home?

(CALPURNIA comes out onto the porch.)

CALPURNIA. Not yet, Mr. Tate. Afternoon, Judge Taylor.

HECK. Cal -- tell him we were passing by. (They nod and are starting off R.)

CALPURNIA. You want him to call?

JUDGE (as they go; pleasantly). We'll be seeing him anyway.

(CALPURNIA re-enters the house, and MISS STEPHANIE CRAWFORD comes on DL.)

JEAN. People moved slowly then -- and somehow it was hotter. A day was twenty-four hours long, but seemed longer. There was no hurry for there was nowhere to go, nothing to buy and no money to buy it with. (MISS STEPHANIE has paused to consider the house at L with disapproval.)

MISS STEPHANIE. Lack of money is no excuse to let a place go like that. At the least they could cut the Johnson grass and rabbit-tobacco. (Turns toward JEAN.) But of course, they're Radleys.

JEAN (identifying). Miss Stephanie Crawford -- a neighborhood scold. According to her, everybody in Maycomb has a streak -- a drinking streak, a gambling streak, a mean streak, a funny streak.

MISS STEPHANIE (emphatically). No Atkinson minds his own business; every third Merriweather is morbid; the truth is not in the Delafields; all the Bufords walk like that; if Mrs. Grace sips gin out of Lydia E. Pinkham bottles, it is nothing unusual -- her mother did the same.

JEAN. She was also your principal source of information about Boo Radley.

MISS STEPHANIE (coming closer; confidentially and with relish). When that boy was in his teens, he took up with some bad ones from Old Sarum. They were arrested on charges of disorderly conduct, disturbing the peace, assault and battery, and using abusive and profane language in the presence and hearing of a female. Boo Radley was released to his father, who shut him up in that house, and he wasn't seen again for fifteen years.

JEAN. I'd have to ask -- as she intended. (To her.) Miss Stephanie, what happened fifteen years later?

MISS STEPHANIE (delighted to continue). Boo Radley was sitting in the living room cutting some items from The Maycomb Tribune to paste in his scrapbook. As his father passed by, Boo drove the scissors into his parent's leg, pulled them out, wiped them on his pants and resumed his activities. Boo was then thirty-three. Mr. Radley said no Radley was going to any insane asylum. So he was kept home, where he is till this day.

JEAN. How do you know? How can you be sure he's still there?

MISS STEPHANIE (as she goes into her house; emphatically). Because I haven't seen him carried out yet. (She exits.)

JEAN (regarding Radley house). Jem and I had never seen him. That didn't come till later, and when it did, we were in no condition to take much notice, being in fear for our lives! (She turns back toward the audience.) People said Boo Radley went out at night when the moon was down. When azaleas froze in a cold snap, it was because he breathed on them. The tall Radley pecan trees shook their fruit into the adjoining schoolyard in the back, but the nuts lay untouched. Radley pecans would kill you. A baseball hit into the Radley yard was a lost ball and no questions asked.

(During this, MRS. DUBOSE has come out onto her porch. She's old and bad-tempered. Supporting herself [partially] with a cane, she crosses to her porch chair which is draped in shawls. JEM, an active boy a few years older than Scout, comes out onto the porch R, holding football.)

JEAN. My brother Jem -- before the fight when his arm got broken. (JEM tucks the football under his arm, plunges off the porch, and starts dodging imaginary tacklers. She smiles.) Alabama must be playing in the Rose Bowl with Jem scoring the winning touchdown.

MRS. DUBOSE (sharply). Where are you going this time of day, Jeremy Finch? Playing hooky, I suppose. I'll just call up the principal and tell him.

JEM. Aw, it's Saturday, Mrs. Dubose.

MRS. DUBOSE. I wonder if your father knows where you are?

JEM. 'Course he does.

MRS. DUBOSE. Maudie Atkinson told me you broke down her scuppernong arbor this morning. She's going to tell your father and then you'll wish you'd never seen the light of day!

JEM (indignant). I haven't been near her scuppernong arbor!

MRS. DUBOSE. Don't you contradict me! (JEM clutches the football as though plunging through center and with MRS. DUBOSE calling after him, bulls his way off L.) If you aren't sent to the reform school before next week, my name's not Dubose! (She starts back into house.)

JEAN. Mrs. Henry Lafayette Dubose. If she was on the porch when Jem or I passed, we'd be raked by her wrathful gaze, subjected to ruthless interrogation regarding our behavior, and given a melancholy prediction on what we'd amount to when we grew up, which was always nothing. Jem and I hated her. We had no idea that she was fighting a hard battle.

(REVEREND SYKES, a Negro minister, dressed conservatively in a black suit, black tie and white shirt, has come on down R.)

REVEREND SYKES (calling). Miss Cal--

(CALPURNIA is coming out onto the porch, followed by SCOUT.)

JEAN. Reverend Sykes of the First Purchase Church -- called First Purchase because it was paid for from the first earnings of the freed slaves.

CALPURNIA. Afternoon, Reverend.

REVEREND SYKES (speaking quietly). It's about Brother Tom Robinson's trouble. We have to do more for his wife and children.

CALPURNIA (agreeing). Yes, Reverend.

REVEREND SYKES. The collection for the next three Sundays will go to Helen. Please encourage everyone to bring what they can.

SCOUT (curiously). Why are you all taking up a collection for Tom Robinson's wife?

REVEREND SYKES. To tell you the truth, Miss Jean Louise, Helen's finding it hard to get work these days.

SCOUT. I know Tom Robinson's done somethin' awful, but why won't folks hire Helen?

REVEREND SYKES. Folks aren't anxious to (Hesitates as he sees someone entering L. He drops his voice.) -- to have anything to do with his family.

(MAYELLA EWELL, a poor girl accustomed to strenuous labor, has entered L on the platform, followed by her father, BOB EWELL, a little bantam cock of a man, ignorant and sharptempered.)

MAYELLA (as they're crossing R). Yes, Pa.

BOB EWELL. I told ya -- stay outa town right now, hear?

MAYELLA (resigned). I hear. (They are continuing off R.)

JEAN (quietly). Bob Ewell -- his daughter, Mayella. No truant officer could keep any of the Ewells in school. No public health officer could free them from filth and disease. Good times or bad, they lived off the county -- in a cabin by the garbage dump near a small Negro settlement. (Smiles. Wryly.) And all Bob Ewell could hold onto that made him feel better than his nearest neighbors was that if scrubbed with lye soap in very hot water -- his skin was white.

SCOUT (puzzled). Why'd you stop talking? Those are just Ewells.

JEAN. Remembering it now, I'm not surprised they stopped talking.

REVEREND SYKES. I have a lot of calls to make. Good-bye, Miss Jean Louise. See you Sunday, Miss Cal.

CALPURNIA (nodding). Reverend.

SCOUT (after him).'Bye. (REVEREND SYKES is crossing L, and exits. Curious.) Cal -- what did Tom Robinson do?

CALPURNIA. You mean, what do they say he did? Old Mr. Bob Ewell accused Tom of attackin' his girl and had him put in jail.

SCOUT (scornfully). But everyone in Maycomb knows the Ewells. You'd think folks would be glad to hire Tom's wife.

CALPURNIA (briefly). That's what you think.

SCOUT (not satisfied). What does it mean -- he attacked her?

CALPURNIA. You'll have to ask Mr. Finch about that. You hungry?

SCOUT (lighting up as she sees someone coming). I have to see Atticus. There's Dill! (CALPURNIA re-enters house.)

JEAN. That was the summer Dill came to us -- Dill, who was to give us the idea of making Boo Radley come out.

(DILL is coming on down L. He's a little older than Scout, small, blond and wise. He's neat, well-dressed with an undercurrent of sophistication, but his laugh is sudden and happy.)

DILL (looking up to SCOUT). Hey.

SCOUT. Hey, Dill. (She starts down from the porch and is crossing toward him.)

JEAN. His real name was Charles Baker Harris, and he'd been sent here to spend the summer with an aunt. We came to know Dill as a pocket Merlin whose head teemed with eccentric plans, strange longings and quaint fancies. He was to be my childhood fiancé -- which was nice for a girl, even if he wasn't very big. "I'm little," he said one time, "but I'm old."

DILL. You watchin' for your father?

SCOUT. That's right. (Struck with sudden curiosity.) What about your daddy?

DILL (cautiously). What do you mean?

(JEM, still carrying the football, is coming back on DL.)

SCOUT. You never say anything about him.

DILL. Because I haven't got one.

SCOUT. Is he dead?

DILL. No.

SCOUT. Then if he isn't dead, you've got one, haven't you? (DILL is embarrassed.)

JEM. Never mind her, Dill.

SCOUT (exasperated). If his father isn't dead, how can he say he hasn't got one?

JEM (has taken her arm). Scout! (She stops at his tone and turns to look with him at the door to the Radley place, which is opening.)

(NATHAN RADLEY, a pale, thin, leathery man is coming out.)

SCOUT (relaxing; softly). Nathan Radley.

JEAN (at R). When old Mr. Radley died some folks thought Boo might come out, but they had another think coming. Boo's older brother, Nathan -- that's him -- moved in and took his father's place. At least Nathan Radley would speak to us. (NATHAN, preoccupied, is passing by.)

JEM (nervously clearing his throat). Hidy do, Mr. Nathan.

NATHAN (walking off). Afternoon.

JEAN (thoughtfully). Looking back for a place to begin -- perhaps it would be what happens next. (She considers this a moment, nods confirmation to herself, and steps off R. Meanwhile SCOUT, JEM and DILL have all turned to look back at the Radley place.)

JEM. Now Boo Radley's in there all by himself.

DILL. Wonder what he does. Looks like he'd stick his head out the door some time.

JEM. He goes out when it's pitch dark. I've seen his tracks in our backyard many a morning, and one night I heard him scratching on the back screen.

DILL. Wonder what he looks like.

JEM (professionally). Judging from his tracks, he's about six and a half feet tall, he eats raw squirrels and any cats he can catch. What teeth he has are yellow and rotten. His eyes pop and most of the time he drools.

DILL (with decision). Let's make him come out.

SCOUT (shocked). Make Boo Radley come out?

JEM. If you want to get yourself killed, all you have to do is go up and knock on that door.

DILL (challenging). You're scared -- too scared to put your big toe in the front yard.

JEM. Ain't scared, just respectful.

DILL. I dare you.

JEM (trapped). You dare me? (He turns to look at the house apprehensively.)

SCOUT. Don't go near it, Jem.

DILL. You gonna run out on a dare?

JEM. Lemme think a minute.

DILL. Just touch the house. I dare you!

JEM. Touch the house, that's all?

DILL. He'll probably come out after you. Then Scout 'n me'll jump on him and hold him down till we can tell him, we just want to look at him. (JEM doesn't respond. Impatiently.) Well?

JEM. Don't hurry me. (He starts slowly toward house.)

DILL. Scout and me's right behind you. (As JEM continues toward the Radley place, they follow, SCOUT pausing beside the tree. As JEM hesitates.) Folks where I come from aren't so scared. I've never seen such scary folks as here. (That does it. JEM speeds to the house, slaps it with his palm, and races back past SCOUT and DILL to R. DILL follows. SCOUT starts to follow, notices something in a knothole in the tree, takes it, and then follows.)

JEM (panting with excitement). So there--- (They all turn and look back at the house.)

DILL (hushed). Someone at the window! Look at the curtains! (The curtains have been pulled slightly to the side, and now they fall back into place.)

JEM (horrified). He was watching! He saw me!

SCOUT (exhausted). Don't _ever_ do that again. (Absently putting a piece of gum in her mouth.) If you get killed -- what with Atticus already so old -- what would become of me?

JEM (considering her). Where'd you get the chewing gum?

SCOUT (as she chews, nodding L). It was sticking in the knothole.

JEM (shocked). That tree? (As she nods.) Spit it out! Right now!

SCOUT (obeying, but indignant). I was just getting the flavor.

JEM (grimly). Suppose Boo Radley put it there? Suppose it's poison? You go gargle!

SCOUT (shaking head). It'd take the taste outa my mouth.

DILL (still concentrating on the Radley house). Let's throw a pebble against the door -- and as soon as he sticks his head out, say we want to buy him an ice cream. (Logically.) That'll seem friendly. Maybe if he came out, and sat a spell with us, he'd feel better.

SCOUT. How do you know he don't feel good now?

DILL (concerned). How'd you feel if you'd been shut up for a hundred years with nothing but cats to eat? (Searching about.) 'Course, if you'd rather _I_ throw the pebble ----

JEM (disgusted). Better leave it to me. (Apparently picking up pebble.) How many times do I have to show you that----

DILL (unimpressed). Maybe you ran up and touched it, but----

SCOUT (worried). You're not going to throw a stone at the Radley house!

JEM (to DILL, as he winds up to throw). I guess I just have to keep on showing you-- (He's stopped by an authoritative voice from off L.)

ATTICUS. Jem! (JEM stops and they all look L.)

DILL. Your father!

SCOUT (at same time). Atticus!

(ATTICUS, carrying an old brief case and wearing his "office" clothes, comes on L. He's tall, quietly impressive, reserved, civilized and nearly fifty. He wears glasses, and because of poor sight in his left eye, looks with his right eye when he wants to see something well.)

ATTICUS (trying to take in the situation; curiously). Just what were you about to do, Jem?

JEM. Nothin', sir.

ATTICUS (he won't be put off). I don't want any of that. Tell me.

JEM. We were ---- (Assuming responsibility.) I was going to throw a pebble -- to get Boo Radley to come out.

ATTICUS. Why?

DILL. Because -- sir. (As ATTICUS turns to him, he finishes lamely.) We thought he might enjoy us.

ATTICUS (gravely). I see. (Turning back to JEM. With decision.) Son, I'm going to tell you something and tell you one time. Don't bother that man.

SCOUT. But why doesn't he ever----

ATTICUS (cutting in). What Mr. Radley does is his own business. If he wants to stay inside his own house, he has the right to stay inside -- free from the attention of inquisitive children. How would you like it if I barged into your rooms at night without knocking?

JEM. That's different.

ATTICUS. Is it?

JEM. Because we're not crazy.

ATTICUS. What Mr. Radley does might seem peculiar to us, but it does not seem peculiar to him.

JEM (protesting). Anyone who stays inside all the time and never ----

ATTICUS (cutting in). But that's his decision. (Considering them.) There's something I'd like to ask. If you'll do it, you'll get along a lot better with all kinds. You see, you never really understand a person until you consider things from his point of view.

JEM. Sir?

ATTICUS. Until you climb into his skin and walk around in it.

JEM (incredulous). You want us to consider things from Boo Radley's point of view?

DILL (impatiently). He means -- everyone.

SCOUT. You stay outa this.

ATTICUS (smiling). Dill's right. But I expect I'm asking too much. (Noticing, L.) There's Walter Cunningham. (With ATTICUS diverted, DILL speaks confidentially to JEM and SCOUT, with a nod toward Radley place.)

DILL. I've got a much better plan. (Starting off L.) See you.

(MR. CUNNINGHAM, a farmer, carrying a sack, is coming on L, as DILL runs off past him.)

ATTICUS (calling). Afternoon, Walter. (Aside to JEM and SCOUT, using Dill's confidential tone and nod.) Regardless of any plans, you're to stay away from that house unless invited.

MR. CUNNINGHAM (holding out sack). This is for you, Mr. Finch. Turnip greens.

ATTICUS (accepting sack gravely). Thank you very much.

MR. CUNNINGHAM. I'd like to pay cash for your services, but between the mortgage and the entailment----

ATTICUS. This is just fine. Jem, please take this sack to Cal. (JEM takes sack and goes inside.) I'd say your bill is settled, Walter.

MR. CUNNINGHAM (doubtfully). You put in a lot of time.

ATTICUS. Let's see now. You left a load of stove wood in the backyard, then a sack of hickory nuts. At Christmas there was a crate of smilax and holly. Now a bag of turnip greens. I'm more than paid.

MR. CUNNINGHAM. If you say so.

SCOUT. Your boy's in my class at school, Mr. Cunningham. (Uneasily, as she recalls.) We had a disagreement the other day.

MR. CUNNINGHAM (smiling). I have a few with that boy myself, little lady.

SCOUT (concerned). I didn't actually beat him up bad.

MR. CUNNINGHAM (amused). If he can't defend himself against a girl, he'll just have to take it. (To ATTICUS. Going.) Much obliged, Mr. Finch.

ATTICUS (after him). Any time I can be of help.

SCOUT (curious). Why does he pay with stove wood and turnip greens?

ATTICUS. Because that's the only way he can.

SCOUT. Are we poor, Atticus?

ATTICUS. We are indeed.

SCOUT. As poor as the Cunninghams?

ATTICUS. Not exactly. The Cunninghams are country folks and the depression hits them hardest. (Curious.) What was your trouble with my client's boy?

SCOUT. He said some things I didn't like. (Shrugs.) I rubbed his nose in the dirt.

ATTICUS. That's not very ladylike. What'd he say?

(JEM is coming back onto porch with his football.)

SCOUT. Things. And I think we should have a talk. I've been watching for you to get home because---- (But she's interrupted by JEM, who is cocking his arm to pass the football.)

JEM. Atticus! Catch!

ATTICUS (making no move). Hang onto it, son. Not today.

JEM (coming down off porch). Atticus, will you be going out for the Methodists? For the football game?

ATTICUS. What game?

JEM (eagerly). It won't be till fall, but everyone's talking about it already. It's for fundraising. The Methodists challenged the Baptists to a game of touch football.

ATTICUS (smiling). Afraid I wouldn't be of much help, Jem.

JEM. Everybody in town's father is playing.

ATTICUS (going up onto porch). Except yours.

JEM (insisting). Every other father----

ATTICUS (cheerfully). I'd break my neck.

JEM. It's touch.

ATTICUS. I'm too old for that sort of thing.

JEM (unhappily; taking breath). Sir -- would you have time to show Scout 'n me how to shoot our air rifles? Later, I mean?

ATTICUS (sorry to be a disappointment). I've told you -- you'll have to wait for your Uncle Jack. (Encouragingly.) He'll <u>really</u> show you.

JEM (ATTICUS seems to be missing the important thing.) Couldn't you show us?

ATTICUS (a simple statement of fact). I'm not interested in guns. (He goes into the house. JEM, disappointed and disturbed, turns back to SCOUT.)

JEM. He's not interested in <u>anything</u>! (With all his strength, Jem throws the football off L.)

SCOUT (unimpressed). Now you'll have to chase after it. (Nodding R. Curious.) Jem -- why do folks slow down as they go past?

JEM (turning). What folks? (He follows the direction of Scout's gaze. Voices are heard from off R.)

VOICE (unfriendly). Yonder's some Finches.

ANOTHER VOICE. Them's his chillun!

ANOTHER VOICE. For all <u>he</u> cares, blacks c'n run loose and rip up the countryside.

SCOUT (perplexed). Why is everybody----

JEM (dismissing them). Because that's the way they are.

SCOUT. But why----

JEM (not wanting to continue; going). I have to get my football.

(As JEM runs off L, ATTICUS comes back onto porch.)

ATTICUS. Someone call?

SCOUT. I've been meaning to ask-- (Takes breath.) Atticus, do you defend niggers?

ATTICUS (startled). Of course I do. Don't say "nigger," Scout. That's common.

SCOUT. 'S what everybody at school says.

ATTICUS. From now on it'll be everybody less one.

SCOUT. Do all lawyers defend N-Negroes?

ATTICUS. They do.

SCOUT (exasperated). Then why do the kids at school make it sound like you're doin' somethin' awful?

ATTICUS. You aren't old enough to understand some things yet, Scout, but there's been a lot of high talk around town that I shouldn't do much about defending Tom Robinson. (Firmly.) But I'm going to defend that man.

SCOUT. If they say you shouldn't, why are you doing it?

ATTICUS (considering this). The main reason -- if I didn't defend him, I couldn't hold my head up. (Looks to SCOUT and smiles.) I couldn't even tell you or Jem not to do something again.

SCOUT. You mean Jem and me wouldn't have to mind you any more?

ATTICUS. That's about right.

SCOUT. Why?

ATTICUS. Because I could never ask you to mind me again. Every lawyer gets at least one case in his lifetime that affects him personally. This one's mine, I guess.

SCOUT. Are we going to win it?

ATTICUS. No, honey.

SCOUT. Then, why--

ATTICUS. Simply because we were licked a hundred years before we started is no reason for us not to try to win.

SCOUT. You sound like some old Confederate veteran.

ATTICUS. Only we aren't fighting Yankees. We'll be fighting our friends. But remember this, no matter how bitter things get, they're still our friends and this is still our home.

SCOUT (confused). Is there something you want me to do, Atticus?

ATTICUS (nodding). Keep your head -- even if things turn ugly. And I hope you can get through what's coming without catching Maycomb's usual disease. Why reasonable people go stark raving mad when anything involving a Negro comes up is something I don't pretend to understand.

SCOUT. The Tom Robinson case must be pretty important.

ATTICUS (speaking quietly). It goes to the essence of a man's conscience.

SCOUT (concerned for him). Suppose you're wrong about it?

ATTICUS. How's that?

SCOUT. Most people think they're right and you're wrong.

ATTICUS. They're entitled to think that, and they're entitled to full respect for their opinions. (Ready to go back into the house.) But before

I can live with other folks, I've got to live with myself.

SCOUT. What does that mean?

ATTICUS (pauses; smiling). One thing doesn't abide by majority rule --
a person's conscience. (ATTICUS goes on into the house. SCOUT looks
after him a moment, then turns and looks off L.)

SCOUT (calling). Jem---- (Eager to talk to him; hurries off L.) Jem --
Hey!

(As SCOUT goes off L. JEAN steps back on R.)

JEAN. I thought I had interesting information to pass along to Jem.
Apparently, our father was more complex than we'd realized. Certainly
this new aspect of his legal practice was more promising than doing
papers in an office. (Shaking head as she recalls.) I found my brother
unresponsive. Probably the Tom Robinson case wasn't quite as new to
him as it was to me. Thinking about it now, probably it was abuse from
older boys that made Jem so eager to involve his father in sensible
community activities -- like a game of touch football. All such invi-
tations were politely declined. Then a few weeks later something
happened -- something that made our father even more of a puzzle. The
tension in the town about the approaching trial was getting drum-tight,
but what happened had nothing to do with that -- it had to do with a
liver-colored bird dog named Tim.

(JEM and SCOUT are coming back in L, with JEM pulling SCOUT
along.)

SCOUT (protesting). Why do I have to come home?

JEM. Because I tell you. (Concerned.) That old dog from down yonder is
sick. (Calling.) Cal, can you come out a minute?

SCOUT. It's only Tim, and he's gone lopsided, that's all.

(CALPURNIA comes out onto porch, wiping hands on a dishcloth.)

CALPURNIA. What is it, Jem? I can't come out every time you want me.

JEM. Somethin' wrong with that old dog down yonder.

CALPURNIA (sighing). I can't wrap up any dog's foot right now.

JEM. He's sick, Cal. Somethin' wrong with him.

CALPURNIA (finally interested). Tryin' to catch his tail?

JEM. No, he's doin' like this. (JEM gulps, like a goldfish, hunching his shoulders and twisting his torso while CALPURNIA watches narrowly.)

CALPURNIA (her voice hardening). You tellin' me a story, Jem Finch?

JEM. No, Cal. And he's coming this way.

CALPURNIA. Runnin'?

JEM (shaking head). Just moseyin' -- but walkin' funny.

CALPURNIA (that decides her). I'll call help. (Pauses before hurrying into house.) You two get in off the street. (She hurries inside.)

JEM (to SCOUT). Come on.

SCOUT (reluctantly coming up onto porch with JEM). He's not even in sight.

CALPURNIA (voice off R, loud and anxious; apparently into telephone). Operator, hello -- Miss Eula May, ma-am? Please gimme Mr. Finch's office -- right away!

SCOUT (to JEM). You started something.

CALPURNIA (off R, half-shouting). Mr. Finch, this is Cal. There's a mad dog down the street a piece. Jem says he's comin' this way! Yes -- yessir -- yes! (Apparently, she hangs up.)

JEM (calling in). What's Atticus say?

CALPURNIA (off R, calling back). In a minute. (Rattling telephone hook, then speaking loudly again.) Miss Eula May. I'm through talking to Mr. Finch. Listen, can you call Miss Crawford, Miss Atkinson and whoever's got a phone on this street and tell 'em a mad dog's comin'? Please, ma-am... hurry!

SCOUT. What about the Radleys? They got a phone?

(CALPURNIA is coming back onto porch.)

JEM. They wouldn't come out anyway.

SCOUT. Maybe Nathan ---- (Starting down off porch toward Radley house.) I better call out to them. (Both CALPURNIA and JEM go after her.)

JEM. No, Scout.

CALPURNIA (catching her). Listen to me -- you go back and you stay.

SCOUT. I just want to shout to the Radleys.

CALPURNIA. You go back! (Then CALPURNIA races up onto the Radley porch where she starts banging on the door, at the same time casting nervous glances L.)

SCOUT (softly; impressed). She's not scared one bit.

JEM (cautiously moving L). I don't see Tim.

SCOUT (following JEM). Maybe he turned off.

JEM. Maybe.

CALPURNIA (meanwhile banging on the Radley door). Mr. Nathan -- Mr. Boo! Mad dog's comin'! Mad dog's comin'! Hear me? Don't come outside. Mad dog! (During this, SCOUT has noticed something in the tree knothole and she takes it.)

JEM (suddenly tense as he watches L). I see him! There he is! Cal! (Grabbing SCOUT.) Get back! (CALPURNIA is running down to join them. She herds them ahead of her with anxious glances back L.)

CALPURNIA. Both of you -- inside the house and stay inside! (Pauses to look back.) That Tim's gone mad all right! (SCOUT has stopped to shout back at the silent Radley place.)

SCOUT. He's comin' now, Mr. Radley!

CALPURNIA (giving SCOUT a fierce swat on the seat). Git inside!

SCOUT (muttering bitterly as she goes up onto porch). You always pick on me.

JEM. You had it coming.

SCOUT (pointing L; justifying). He's moving slow as a snail. (They've all turned on the porch to watch L. SCOUT starts inspecting a small box she's holding.)

JEM. What's that?

SCOUT. Finders-keepers.

JEM (watching L again). Where'd you find it?

SCOUT. Where I found the chewing gum -- that old knothole.

JEM (startled into looking at SCOUT again). The Radley tree? (SCOUT shrugs her indifference.)

CALPURNIA (watching intently; softly). Please come soon, Mr. Finch.

JEM. What's inside?

SCOUT (inspecting). Two pennies -- all slicked up

JEM (impressed). Indian-heads. They're real valuable. They make you have good luck. Why would someone leave valuable Indian-head pennies----

SCOUT (protectively). They're mine. (Pointing L.) I risked my life out there!

JEM (considering the situation off L again). Old Tim's walkin' like his right legs are shorter than his left legs. (They all lean forward to watch. From off R there's the sound of an automobile approaching.)

JEAN. We assumed that Atticus would turn to competent authority to handle this dangerous situation, and our assumption was to prove correct. (The sound of the approaching car comes to a stop.) When our father arrived, he was accompanied by the sheriff.

(ATTICUS comes on down R with HECK TATE, who carries a heavy rifle. They go past JEAN as though she isn't there and pause by the far edge of the porch.)

JEM (starting down to join them). Atticus -- he's over there behind...

ATTICUS. Stay on the porch, son.

CALPURNIA. Back behind the Radley pecan trees.

HECK. Not runnin', is he, Cal?

CALPURNIA. He's in the twitchin' stage, Mr. Heck.

HECK (watching carefully as he advances a few steps toward L). Usually they go in a straight line, but you never can tell.

ATTICUS (following behind HECK toward down C). The slope will probably bring him back onto the road.

SCOUT (to CALPURNIA). I thought mad dogs foamed at the mouth and jumped at your throat.

CALPURNIA. Hush.

ATTICUS (softly). There he is.

SCOUT. He just looks sick.

HECK (aside to ATTICUS). He's got it all right, Mr. Finch.

JEM (calling). Is he looking for a place to die, Mr. Heck?

HECK (over his shoulder). Far from dead, Jem. He hasn't got started yet.

ATTICUS. He's within range, Heck. You better get him before he goes down a side street. Lord knows who's around the corner. (Calling back.) Cal----

CALPURNIA (understanding; to JEM and SCOUT). Inside the house -- both of you.

JEM (temporizing). If he gets closer.

SCOUT (clutching porch rail tightly with both hands). I don't go in till he goes in.

JEM. I wanta watch the sheriff!

JEAN. It was right then -- the most astonishing thing happened. Jem and I almost fainted!

HECK (turning; offering rifle to ATTICUS). You take him, Mr. Finch. You do it.

JEAN. We thought the sheriff must've lost his mind.

ATTICUS (urgently). Don't waste time, Heck! Go on!

HECK. Mr. Finch -- this is a one-shot job.

ATTICUS (vehemently). Don't just stand there, Heck!

HECK (frantic). Look where he is! For God's sake, Mr. Finch! I can't shoot that well and you know it.

ATTICUS. I haven't shot a gun in thirty years.

HECK (shoving rifle into Atticus' hands). I'd feel mighty comfortable if you did now. (Holding the rifle, ATTICUS looks L. He decides to accept the responsibility and, watching carefully, he moves several steps to the L.)

JEAN (as this is happening). Jem and I were in a fog -- watching our father standing there in the street with a rifle. Others were watching, too, but we didn't know it then. It didn't make any sense at all. It was utterly beyond belief. (ATTICUS has taken off his glasses, still watching L, and drops them on the street. He rubs one eye and blinks. Then his body goes tense as he focuses totally on the mad dog off L.)

CALPURNIA (her hands to her cheeks). Sweet Jesus, help him. (ATTICUS works the bolt action, apparently slamming a cartridge into the chamber, raises the rifle quickly, and apparently fires. Sound effect from off stage.)

HECK (a shout). Got him! (Happy and relieved, as he hurries off L.) You got him!

ATTICUS (after him). Yes, but I think I was a little to the right. (Muttering as he picks up his glasses.) If I had my druthers, I'd take a shotgun!

(HECK is re-entering L.)

HECK. Dead as a doornail. (As though it's news.) Just a little to the right.

ATTICUS (handing rifle back to HECK). Always was.

(Porch doors are opening, and MISS STEPHANIE and MISS MAUDIE are cautiously coming out.)

HECK. I'll have someone come down with a pickup and take him away.

ATTICUS (stopping JEM and SCOUT, who are starting down off porch). You stay where you are.

HECK. You haven't forgot much, Mr. Finch. They say it never leaves you.

JEM (calling). Atticus--

ATTICUS. Yes, Jem?

JEM. I -- I didn't know----

MISS MAUDIE (from her porch). I saw that, One-Shot Finch. (ATTICUS shakes his head at her and turns back to his son.)

ATTICUS. Jem -- you and your sister stay away from that dog. He's just as dangerous dead as alive.

JEM. Yes, sir. Atticus?

ATTICUS. What, son?

HECK (amused at Jem's hesitation). What's the matter, boy, can't you talk? Didn't you know your daddy's--

ATTICUS. Hush, Heck. (Starting R.) Let's get back to town.

HECK. What's your hurry now? (Good-humored teasing.) Have to get back to workin' up your speeches for the trial?

ATTICUS (as they go; wryly). Don't remind me. (They go out R. CALPURNIA goes inside.)

MISS STEPHANIE. Maybe Tim wasn't really mad. Maybe he was just full of fleas -- and Atticus Finch shot him dead.

MISS MAUDIE. If that Tim was still comin' up the street, maybe you'd be singing a different tune.

MISS STEPHANIE (agreeing). Maybe I would. (As she's going back into the house.) I'll admit I felt safer when I saw Atticus take the rifle.

JEM (still in shock). Did you see him, Scout? All of a sudden it looked like that gun was a part of him. He did it so quick -- I hafta aim for ten minutes 'fore I can hit somethin'.

MISS MAUDIE (with a wicked smile). Well, now, Miss Jean Louise. Still think your father can't do anything? Still ashamed of him?

SCOUT (meekly). No, ma'am.

MISS MAUDIE. Forgot to mention the other day that he was the deadest shot in Maycomb County.

JEM. Dead shot--

MISS MAUDIE. Something for you to think about, Jem Finch. When he was a boy his nickname was Ol' One-Shot. Why, if he shot fifteen times and hit fourteen doves, he'd complain about wasting ammunition.

JEM. But he never said anything about it.

SCOUT. Wonder why he never goes huntin' now.

MISS MAUDIE. If your father's anything, he's civilized. Marksmanship like that's a gift of God. I think maybe he put his gun down when he realized God had given him an unfair advantage.

SCOUT. Looks like he'd be proud of it.

MISS MAUDIE (going). People like your father never bother about pride in their gifts. (She re-enters her house.)

JEAN. This bewildering event unsettled our established view of Atticus. It was something to talk over -- no, celebrate! (Wryly.) But we didn't get far.

(MRS. DUBOSE is coming out onto her porch.)

SCOUT (filled with anticipation). Will I have something to tell 'em at school on Monday!

JEM. Don't know if we should say anything about it.

SCOUT (going down off porch). I'd like to find the Cunningham boy right now! Ain't everybody's daddy the deadest shot in Maycomb County.

JEM (following her). I reckon if he'd wanted us to know, he'd a told us.

SCOUT. Maybe it just slipped his mind.

JEM. Naw, it's something you wouldn't understand. (Blazing with this new pride.) We don't have to talk about it any more'n he does -- but we know! (To the sky.) An' I don't care if he's a hundred years old!

SCOUT (calling out). Hey, Mrs. Dubose! Did you see my father----

MRS. DUBOSE. Don't say "hey" to me, you ugly girl! You say "good afternoon, Mrs. Dubose."

JEAN. In point of fact Jem and I didn't get to the end of the street before we'd been slapped down again about our father.

MRS. DUBOSE. You should be in a dress and camisole, young lady. If somebody doesn't change your ways, you'll grow up waiting on tables. A Finch waiting on tables at the O.K. Cafe -- hah! (SCOUT, upset, reaches out and takes Jem's hand.)

JEAN. I was terrified. The O. K. Cafe was a dim organization at the edge of town. (As she recalls.) We still didn't know what was really the matter with Mrs. Dubose -- but that's part of what Atticus wanted us to do -- part of why I'm trying to remember it all now. (JEAN steps off R. Meanwhile JEM has disentangled his hand from that of his uneasy sister.)

JEM (aside to her; whispering). Come on, Scout. Don't pay any attention. Just hold your head high -- and be a gentleman. (SCOUT decides to make the effort, and they start L again. However, MRS. DUBOSE won't let them alone.)

MRS. DUBOSE. A lovelier lady than your mother never lived. It's shocking the way Atticus Finch lets her children run wild.

SCOUT (as JEM hesitates; whispering). I'm with you.

JEM (whispering back). We'll keep walking.

MRS. DUBOSE. Not only a Finch waiting on tables, but one in the courthouse, lawing for niggers! (JEM, stung hard, stops short.)

SCOUT (whispering, anxiously). Let's keep goin', Jem.

MRS. DUBOSE (as she's going back inside). What's this world come to with the Finches going against their raising? (Her parting shot.) Your

father's no better than the trash he works for! (With this, she completes
her exit, leaving SCOUT hurt and JEM stunned.)

JEM (gasping). I'll -- I'll fix her!

SCOUT. Hold your head high, Jem, an'----

JEM. She has no right----

SCOUT (trying to hold him). Jem----

JEM (shoving her hands away). Just because Atticus -- I'm sick and tired
-- everybody---- (He races up onto Mrs. Dubose's porch, where he starts
tearing up the potted flowers there.)

SCOUT (frantic). Jem! Come back!

JEM (shouting back). Go home! Stay outa this (As the shocked SCOUT
feels her way back toward her porch, JEM turns, having completed the
destruction of Mrs. Dubose's porch flowers, and rushes off back,
apparently intent on further objects for his fury.)

SCOUT (after him; a cry). Jem! (But JEM, past hearing, has gone.)

(Frightened, SCOUT goes back onto her porch, from where she watches
anxiously UL. DILL, dressed in different clothes -- dusty and mussed
-- comes on DR.)

DILL (subdued). Hey, Scout.

SCOUT (Dill's presence only half-registering). Jem's outa control! He's
gone mad! (Looking back UL.) He's knocking the tops off every
camellia bush Mrs. Dubose owns!

DILL (impressed). Thought Jem had a slow fuse.

SCOUT. Not any more. He's gone crazy.

DILL. From people sayin' things about your father?

SCOUT. Yes -- Mrs. Dubose---- (Stops herself; curiously.) How'd you
know? (DILL shrugs. Eager for DILL to know.) We found out
somethin' about Atticus today -- somethin' special.

DILL (not surprised). About time.

SCOUT (bursting with it). He's the deadest shot in Maycomb!

DILL (this isn't what he expects; disappointed). That's what you found
out?

SCOUT (nodding). It's the truth. So it doesn't matter what folks say.

DILL. Wouldn't matter anyway. (SCOUT becomes aware that they' re not quite talking about the same thing. She considers him.)

SCOUT. What are you doing here? I thought you'd been taken back to stay with your folks in Meridian?

DILL (uneasily). I -- I was.

SCOUT. Then how in the Sam Hill----

DILL. It's -- you see----

SCOUT (as his appearance finally registers). You're all mussed 'n' dusty.

DILL (plunging). 'Course I am. (Takes a quick breath.) I have a new father, and he doesn't like me -- so he had me bound in chains and left to die in the basement. But I was secretly kept alive on raw field beans by a passing farmer who heard my cries for help.

SCOUT. If you were chained up in the basement----

DILL. The good man poked a bushel of beans to me -- pod by pod -- through the ventilator!

(During this, JEM is coming back on where he went off. Aghast at himself, he's moving slowly toward the porch, not yet noticed by the others.)

SCOUT (hooked). Lucky for you that good man was passing.

DILL (sure of himself now). I worked myself free -- pulling the chains from the walls. Then -- still in wrist irons -- I wandered out of Meridian where I discovered a small animal show -- and they hired me to wash the camel.

SCOUT. How do you go about washing a----

DILL (pressing on). I traveled all over with that show-- everywhere -- till suddenly my sense of direction told me I was just across the river from Maycomb. (Gulps a quick breath.) What I did then-- (JEM has come up on the last of this, still unnoticed.)

JEM (cutting in). How did you get here, Dill?

DILL. Hey, Jem.

SCOUT. Jem — (Suddenly it comes back. Horrified.) Jem -- what did you —

JEM (cutting her off). I was speaking to Dill.

DILL (sighing; undramatic).   I took thirteen dollars from my mother's purse, caught the nine o'clock train from Meridian, got off at the junction, and walked the rest of the way.

JEM. Why'd you run off?

DILL. Didn't run off. Decided I'd come back here, that's all.

SCOUT. You want to stay with your Aunt Rachel?

DILL. I want to stay here.

SCOUT. With us?

JEM (grim). We're gonna have a hot summer.

DILL. I don't care.

(ATTICUS is hurrying on DR.)

SCOUT (warning). Jem---- (ATTICUS walks past them over to in front of the Dubose place, and for a moment he considers it.)

JEM (aside to DILL; nervously). Maybe you better come back later.

DILL (hushed). I'm not going. (ATTICUS turns and starts back toward group at R.)

SCOUT (bravely). Look at this, Atticus -- we've got a visitor. Here's Dill -- come back from Meridian. (Trying to fill awkward silence.) He knows how to wash a camel.

ATTICUS (gravely acknowledging). Dill.

DILL (swallowing). Sir.

ATTICUS (a suggestion of winter in his voice). Jem -- I had a phone call a few minutes ago. Are you responsible for the damage to those flowers?

JEM. Yes, sir.

ATTICUS. Why'd you do it?

JEM (softly). Mrs. Dubose said you lawed for niggers.

ATTICUS (getting it straight). And that's why you destroyed her garden?

JEM (swallowing). Yes, sir.

ATTICUS. Son, I have no doubt you've been annoyed by your contemporaries about me lawing for niggers, as you say, but to do something like this to a sick old lady is inexcusable. I strongly advise you to go over and have a talk with Mrs. Dubose.

JEM (startled). Talk to her!

ATTICUS. Right now.

JEM. But----

ATTICUS. Go on, Jem.

SCOUT. But -- sir----

ATTICUS (stopping her). Scout.

JEM (getting himself together). All right. I'll go talk to her.

ATTICUS (unmoved). Come straight home afterwards. (JEM starts for the Dubose house like a man walking bravely to his execution. During the following speeches, he goes up to her door, knocks, and is let in.)

SCOUT (to ATTICUS). All he was doin' was standin' up for you!

ATTICUS (as he looks after JEM). Never thought Jem'd be the one to lose his head. (Turning.) Thought I'd have more trouble with you.

SCOUT. Why do we have to keep our heads anyway? Nobody at school has to keep his head about anything.

ATTICUS (not happy about it). You'll soon have to be keeping your head about far worse things. (Turning to DILL.) Your Aunt Rachel didn't mention you were coming back.

SCOUT. She doesn't know.

DILL. Please, Mr. Finch -- don't tell her I'm here.

ATTICUS. Don't tell her----

SCOUT. He's run away.

DILL. Don't make me go back, sir!

ATTICUS. Just let me get this straight----

DILL. If you make me go back, I'll run away again.

ATTICUS. Whoa, son.

SCOUT. He's been living on raw beans.

DILL (nervously). Scout----

ATTICUS. Let me do a little telephoning. (Not letting DILL interrupt.) I'll ask if you could spend the night -- perhaps stay a few days.

DILL (hopefully). Would you, sir?

ATTICUS (as he goes inside). Maybe Scout can get you something to go with the raw beans.

DILL (after him). Oh, I'm fine. Not hungry at all. (ATTICUS smiles as he enters house.)

SCOUT (regarding DILL critically). I'd think you'd be starving. (DILL shrugs. Scout's suspicions are growing.) Was your father really hateful like you said?

DILL (unhappy). That wasn't it, he -- they just wasn't interested in me.

SCOUT. You're not telling me right. Your folks couldn't do without you.

DILL. Yes, they can. They get on a lot better without me. They stay gone most of the time, and when they're home, they're always off by themselves. And -- I can't help them any. (Being fair.) They're not mean. They buy me everything I want, but then it's---- (Imitating man's voice.) -- now-you've-got-it-go-play-with-it.

SCOUT. They must need you. Why, Atticus couldn't get along a day without my help and advice.

DILL (struggling with an idea). The special thing about your father -- it isn't that he's a dead shot, it's----

SCOUT (highly critical). He made Jem go over to Mrs. Dubose.

DILL. Don't you see why he did that?

SCOUT (unimpressed). Because it's his way.

DILL (agreeing). And Jem'll be all right. (Trying to catch her interest.) If I get to stay a few days, I have a new plan for bringing out Boo Radley.

SCOUT (turning to look at Radley house). Why do you reckon Boo Radley's never run off?

DILL. Maybe he doesn't have anywhere to run off to. (Back to business.) For my plan, we'll need a box of lemon drops. I'll put one just outside his door -- and then a row of them down the street.

(ATTICUS is coming back onto the porch, but DILL is too wrapped up in his scheme to see him.)

DILL. When he thinks he's safe, he'll come out to pick up the lemon drop. (His pantomiming is leading him toward the still unseen ATTICUS.) Then he'll notice the next one -- then on to the next -- he'll follow like an ant -- then another -- then---- (The place for the next piece of imaginary candy is occupied by Atticus's shoes. DILL stops and looks up.)

ATTICUS (smiling). That's a lot of lemon drops.

DILL (uneasily). We were foolin', sir.

ATTICUS. You've been the subject of considerable conversation.

DILL. What'd Aunt Rachel say?

ATTICUS. At first it came under the heading of "Wait till they get you home." Then it was "His folks must be out of their minds worrying." She went on to "That's all the Harris in him coming out," and she ended with "Reckon he can stay on for tonight anyway. "

DILL (delighted). Hey! (To SCOUT.) Hear that!

ATTICUS. But I thought I'd better speak to your parents, so I called them, too.

DILL (suddenly serious). What'd they say?

ATTICUS. Couldn't 've been more agreeable. (Smiles.) They said you could stay on for as long as you're not in the way. (SCOUT gives a gasp of pleasure.)

DILL (subdued). I see.

SCOUT. Great! Isn't that great?

DILL (with an effort). Sure is. (To ATTICUS. Fishing.) Guess they were looking all over Meridian for me.

ATTICUS (shaking head, smiling). No, they thought you were probably stuck at some picture show.

DILL (disappointed, but smiling back). Generally, they'd be right, too.

ATTICUS (coming aware of Dill's problem). We'll be going through quite a difficult time, Dill. It'll be good having you with us.

DILL. Do you mean----

ATTICUS. It'll be a help having you here. There's a cot in Jem's room.

(HECK TATE is coming on L.)

DILL. Thank you, sir. Thank you very much.

HECK (calling). Mr. Finch.

ATTICUS. More company. Come on up, Heck.

HECK (reserved). Rather speak with you down here.

ATTICUS (thoughtfully). Oh?

SCOUT (aside to her father). What is it?

ATTICUS. Only two reasons why grown men talk in the front yard --

death or politics. (Calling.) Which is it, Heck?

HECK (wryly). Could be a little of both, Mr. Finch.

ATTICUS (considering this). Then we'd better talk. (Pauses. To SCOUT.) Maybe you and Dill can give Calpurnia a hand.

SCOUT. I want to know what's happening.

ATTICUS (firmly). You'll stay here. (Glancing toward him.) Dill? (DILL takes hold of Scout's arm, as ATTICUS crosses to HECK.)

SCOUT (jerking arm free). Don't get any idea you can boss me, too! (She crosses to porch swing.)

DILL (following apologetic). They have business. (HECK has turned aside and speaks confidentially to ATTICUS.)

HECK. They moved Tom Robinson to the county jail this afternoon. I don't look for trouble, but I can't guarantee there won't be any.

ATTICUS. Don't be foolish, Heck. This is Maycomb.

HECK. I'm just uneasy, that's all.

ATTICUS. Trial'll probably begin day after tomorrow. You can keep him till then, can't you? (Smiling.) I don't think anybody'll begrudge me a client with times this hard.

HECK (smiling back). It's just that Old Sarum bunch. You know how they do when they get shinnied up.

ATTICUS. Are they drinking?

HECK. Could be. (Worried.) I don't see why you touched this case. You've got everything to lose.

ATTICUS (quietly). Do you really think so? (At this, SCOUT comes to porch rail followed by DILL.)

HECK (taking breath; frankly). Yes, I do, Atticus. I mean -- everything.

ATTICUS (with decision). Heck, that boy might go to the chair, but he's not going till the truth's told.

HECK (resigned). Okay, Mr. Finch.

ATTICUS. And you know as well as I do what the truth is.

(JEM, coming from the Dubose house, pauses as he sees HECK and his father.)

HECK (withdrawn). Just thought I should keep you informed.

ATTICUS. And I appreciate it, Heck. Thank you.

HECK (relaxing again as he starts L). Sure---- Well, take care of yourself.

ATTICUS (after him; smiling). Don't worry. (As JEM approaches.) Well, son?

JEM. I told her I'd work on her garden and try to make it grow back. And I said I was sorry -- but I'm not. (Gestures L.) What was Heck Tate----

ATTICUS (cutting in). No point in saying you're sorry, if you aren't.

JEM. How about what she said?

ATTICUS. She's old and she's ill. (Starting back into house.) I have work.

JEM (after him). She wants me to read to her. (ATTICUS pauses.) She wants me to come over every afternoon and read out loud for two hours. Atticus -- do I have to?

ATTICUS. You do.

JEM (protesting). Her house is so dark -- creepy -- shadows on the ceiling.

ATTICUS (smiling grimly). That should appeal to your imagination. (Going.) Just pretend you're inside the Radley house. (JEM looks after ATTICUS.)

JEM (perplexed). He's sure in a peculiar mood these days. (Turning.) What'd Heck want?

DILL (dramatic). Death and politics!

SCOUT. Don't be silly. It was just they moved Tom Robinson to the Maycomb jail.

DILL (to JEM). Your father said I could stay. He said I could take the cot in your room.

SCOUT. What are you gonna read to Mrs. Dubose?

JEM. Ivanhoe. (Perplexed.) Why would she want me to read aloud?

DILL. Seemed like your father wasn't surprised.

(ATTICUS is coming back onto the porch with CALPURNIA. He's carrying a small folding chair and an electrical extension cord with a light bulb at the end.)

JEM (anxiously, to DILL). Why wouldn't he be surprised?

DILL. Ask him.

ATTICUS. Ask me what?

JEM. Nothin'.

ATTICUS. You folks'll be in bed when I come back, so I'll say good night now.

SCOUT. Where are you goin'?

ATTICUS. Out. You mind Calpurnia.

JEM. What are you doin' with the chair and light bulb?

ATTICUS. Might have use for them. (Going.) Look after things, Cal.

CALPURNIA. Do my best, Mr. Finch. (ATTICUS is going off L.)

SCOUT (turning to CALPURNIA). Where's he goin'?

CALPURNIA (looking after ATTICUS; a bit grim). I could make a guess -- only I won't. Almost time for dinner. You get washed -- all three of you. (CALPURNIA goes back inside.)

DILL. I really need a wash.

SCOUT. That's the main thing Cal thinks about. Why wouldn't she make a guess? (No one has an answer.)

JEM. Why was Atticus takin' a chair an' a light bulb? (No one has the answer to that either, and they start inside. As they go:) What else was Heck sayin' to Atticus?

(As they go inside, JEAN comes on DR. The lights begin slowly dimming, and an inner curtain is lowered or comes across at the top of the second level of the stage and immediately in front of the upper level porches and the Radley house. Then ATTICUS enters L on the second level just in front of the curtain. He comes to ULC carrying a standing hat rack which he sets up, and over which he hangs the light bulb, the cord to which goes off L. Then he sets up his folding chair beside this.)

JEAN (meanwhile). Dill and I recounted all we'd heard of the conversation in the yard, and Jem thought about it. He hardly said a word through dinner. Then, later, instead of going to bed, Jem said he thought he'd go downtown for a while. I decided I was coming, too -- and there was no stopping Dill. (The stage is now much darker.) We crept past Mrs. Dubose's house -- the Radley place -- and then on to the town square. It was deserted. We thought Atticus was probably in his office, and we went over -- but he wasn't. We were getting uneasy.

(SCOUT, JEM and DILL are coming on DR and they go a few steps past JEAN, not seeing her, and then stop.)

JEAN. We came around by the courthouse and when we did, we noticed something peculiar -- there was a light over the door to the jailhouse. (ATTICUS has meanwhile seated himself in his chair, opened his newspaper, and turned on the light bulb [very low power] hanging beside him, and is reading.)

JEM (relieved). There he is!

SCOUT (starting). Well, let's----

JEM (grabbing her). No, Scout.

SCOUT. I just want to ask why he's sitting in front of the jailhouse.

DILL. Maybe we shouldn't bother him right now.

SCOUT. But----

DILL. It's pretty late.

JEM. He's all right, so let's go home. I just wanted to see where he was. (The sound of approaching cars begins.)

SCOUT. After all this runnin' round town, we might at least----

JEM. Shh-----

SCOUT. He can't hear me.

JEM. No -- listen!

DILL. It's cars. A lotta cars coming. (The sound is getting closer, and then it stops.)

JEM (nervously). I wonder what----

DILL. So many.

JEM (hushed; urgent). Get down. We'll get down 'n' watch. (They get down to watch unseen. The stage light is quite dim now except for the small area around ATTICUS, who has meanwhile looked up at the sound. He closes his newspaper, folds it and puts it in his lap. Then he pushes his hat back on his head, waiting.)

SCOUT (a half-scared whisper). What's happening?

JEM (whispering back). Quiet!

JEAN. The way it looked to us, Atticus was quite calm. He seemed to be expecting exactly what was coming.

(In the darkness, a group of men come on L, seen only dimly, moving slowly and deliberately toward ATTICUS. The group includes MR. CUNNINGHAM and BOB EWELL, and if extras are not available, the rest of the "mob" can be made up of the other male members of the cast. They are not identifiable in the dim light, all dressed in farm clothes. They are facing toward ATTICUS and away from the audience. They are sullen, determined and ominous.)

BOB EWELL. He in there, Mr. Finch?

ATTICUS. He is, and he's asleep. Don't wake him up.

MR. CUNNINGHAM. You know what we want. Step aside from the door, Mr. Finch.

ATTICUS. You can turn around and go home again, Walter.

MR. CUNNINGHAM. Won't do that.

ATTICUS (pleasantly). Might as well. Heck Tate's around somewhere.

BOB EWELL. The hell he is.

THIRD MAN. Heck's bunch's so deep in the woods, they won't get out till morning.

ATTICUS. Indeed? Why so?

THIRD MAN. Called 'em off on a snipe hunt.

BOB EWELL (crowing). Didn't you think o' that, Mr. Finch?

ATTICUS. Thought about it, but didn't believe it.

MR. CUNNINGHAM. Guess that changes things.

BOB EWELL. Oh, yes, it do!

ATTICUS (getting up from his chair). Do you really think so? (At this, SCOUT is getting up. ATTICUS and the group face each other.)

JEAN. "Do you really think so?" was a dangerous question from Atticus. I decided he was about to deal with somebody. This was too good to miss!

SCOUT. I'm gonna see---- (She darts forward.)

JEM (after her; anxiously). Scout! Wait! (But SCOUT rushes through the group, and up to the second level.)

SCOUT (as she comes). H--ey, Atticus!

ATTICUS (startled; afraid for her). Scout! (JEM and DILL are following into the circle of light.)

JEM (apologetic). Couldn't hang onto her.

ATTICUS (urgently). Go home, Jem. Take Scout and Dill and go home. (But JEM is looking at the group.) Jem -- I said, go home.

JEM (back to ATTICUS). Will you be coming with us?

ATTICUS. Son, I told you---- (A big man grabs JEM.)

BIG MAN. I'll send him home.

SCOUT. Don't you touch him!

BIG MAN. I'm telling you to---- (SCOUT kicks the big man in the shins, and he cries out, letting go of JEM and hopping back into the group.)

ATTICUS. That'll do, Scout. Don't kick folks.

SCOUT (indignant). But he----

ATTICUS. No, Scout.

SCOUT. Nobody gonna do Jem that way.

THIRD MAN. All right, Mr. Finch, you get 'em outa here.

BOB EWELL. Give ya fifteen seconds.

JEM. I ain't going.

ATTICUS. Please, Jem, take them and go.

JEM (grimly determined). No, sir. (The crowd is stirring with impatience.)

CROWD (muttering; angry). Had about enough -- the kids are his worry--- Can't stand around all night -- come on -- get 'em outa the way and -- (But the last speaker is interrupted as SCOUT thinks she recognizes a man in front.)

SCOUT. Mr. Cunningham -- that you? (Coming closer.) Hey, Mr. Cunningham. (He doesn't reply. The others are watching. SCOUT is more confused.) Don't you remember me? I'm Jean Louise Finch. You brought us a big bag of turnip greens, remember?

ATTICUS (perplexed). Scout----

SCOUT (struggling for recognition). I go to school with your boy, Walter. Well, he's your boy, ain't he? Ain't he, sir? (MR. CUNNINGHAM is moved to a small nod. SCOUT is relieved.) Knew he was your boy. Maybe he told you about me -- because I beat him up one time -- but he was real nice about it. Tell Walter "hey" for me, won't you? (There's no reply. She tries harder to break through this baffling lack of response.) My father was telling me about your entailment. He said they're bad. (The lack of response is getting more disturbing.) Atticus

-- I was just sayin' to Mr. Cunningham that entailments are bad -- but I remember you said not to worry -- it takes long sometimes -- but you'd all ride it out together. (SCOUT has come to a stop looking out at the silent men. She swallows.) What is it? Can't anybody tell me? (A plea.) Mr. Cunningham -- what's the matter? (Suddenly MR. CUNNINGHAM puts his hands on both of Scout's shoulders.)

MR. CUNNINGHAM. Ain't nothin' the matter, little lady. An' I'll tell my boy you said "hey." (With this, he straightens up and waves his hand. With authority.) Let's clear out of here, boys. (There's a moment of hesitation.) Hard. We're goin' home. (With this, the men start moving off L.)

JEM (hushed with astonishment). They're goin'!

ATTICUS (a bit astonished himself). Looks that way.

SCOUT (going up to him). Atticus -- can <u>we</u> go home now? (ATTICUS takes out a handkerchief with which he wipes his face, and then blows his nose.)

ATTICUS (nodding). Yes. Looks like we can go home now. (There's the sound of cars starting up and driving away. They look off L at the sound.)

JEM. I thought Mr. Cunningham was a friend.

ATTICUS. Still is. He just has his blind spots along with the rest of us.

JEM. But he was ready to hurt you.

ATTICUS. Because he was a part of a mob. But a mob's always made up of people, and Mr. Cunningham's still a man. What you children did -- you made him remember that.

(A soft husky voice, that of TOM ROBINSON, calls from behind.)

TOM (from the darkness). Mr. Finch? (They turn.) They gone?

ATTICUS. They're gone, Tom. They won't bother you any more.

TOM (voice only). Thank you, Mr. Finch.

ATTICUS. We're going to have a busy time. Better get your sleep.

TOM (wryly humorous). You better get some sleep, too.

ATTICUS (smiling as he gathers his things together). That's my intention. Good night, Tom. (DILL has come up to ATTICUS.)

DILL (respectfully). Can I carry the chair for you, Mr. Finch?

ATTICUS (considers, then hands folded chair to DILL). Why, thank you, son. (DILL is deeply pleased.)

SCOUT (drained). I want to go home.

ATTICUS (affectionately gripping Jem's shoulder with one hand and Scout's with the other). You two certainly don't mind very well.

SCOUT (puzzled). Atticus -- what was it you said we did to Mr. Cunningham?

ATTICUS. You made him stand in my shoes for a minute. (With this, ATTICUS reaches up and turns out the light bulb, and in the darkness they exit L.)

(Meanwhile, the only light on the stage is a dim spot on JEAN at DR. As she speaks, the light comes up on the rest of the stage as the courtroom is set up.)

JEAN. The following Monday, Atticus told us to stay home, and for a while we did. People were streaming into town like it was Saturday. Seemed like the whole county was coming for Tom Robinson's trial.

(As the light comes up, it's seen that another inner curtain now covers the fence and tree by the Radley house.

Members of the cast -- or stagehands -- are moving on the basic props for the courtroom. The judge's bench and chair are placed down L with a witness chair just upstage and to the right. There's a bench for witnesses at ULC. To the right of this, there's a small table and chair, and at URC there's another table with two chairs. As the scene is played, the jury is considered out in the audience. As JEAN continues, JUDGE TAYLOR takes his place behind the bench. HECK TATE sits in the witness chair. BOB EWELL and MAYELLA EWELL sit in the bench at ULC, while ATTICUS and TOM ROBINSON sit at the table URC. MR. GILMER is standing to the side of the witness chair.

Spectators come on at the upper level, carrying small folding chairs which they set up and sit on to watch the trial. To the left on the upper level are MISS CRAWFORD, MISS ATKINSON, NATHAN RADLEY and MR. CUNNINGHAM. There's an open space on the upper level, and HELEN ROBINSON sits by herself and away from the white spectators.)

JEAN (continuing during above). When Jem, Dill and I reached the courthouse square, we found it covered with picnic parties. Apparently, the trial was to be a gala occasion. There was no room at the public hitching rail -- mules and wagons were parked under every available tree. People were washing down biscuit and syrup with warm milk from fruit jars. Some were gnawing on cold chicken and cold fried pork chops. In the far corner of the square, the Negroes sat quietly in the sun, dining on sardines and crackers. At some invisible signal, they all got up and started into the courthouse. We didn't want Atticus to see us, so we waited. Then, there were no seats left. Reverend Sykes asked if we'd care to sit on the colored side of the balcony. Jem said, "gosh, yes" and we went in with him.

(SCOUT, JEM and DILL are coming on during this with REVEREND SYKES, and they sit to the right with HELEN ROBINSON. REVEREND SYKES gives her a reassuring pat, but she just stares forward.)

JEAN. By the time we got there the trial was already started. The prosecutor, a Mr. Gilmer from Abbottsville, was taking testimony from Heck Tate. (JEAN steps off R.)
MR. GILMER. In your own words, Mr. Tate.
HECK (replying to MR. GILMER). Well, I was called----
MR. GILMER (motioning toward audience). Could you say it to the jury, Mr. Tate? Who called you?
HECK (turning toward audience). I was fetched by Bob -- by Mr. Bob Ewell yonder, one night.
MR. GILMER. What night, sir?
HECK. The night of November twenty-first. I was leaving my office to go

home when B---- Mr. Ewell came in, very excited he was, and said, get to his house quick, some N-Negro'd attacked his girl. (REVEREND SYKES sighs. HELEN ROBINSON closes her eyes with pain.)

MR. GILMER. Did you go?

HECK. Certainly. Got in the car and went out as fast as I could.

MR. GILMER. And what did you find?

HECK. Found her lying on the floor. She was pretty well beat up, but I heaved her to her feet and she washed her face in the bucket, and she said she was all right.

MR. GILMER. Go on.

HECK. I asked her who hurt her and she said it was Tom Robinson. (JUDGE TAYLOR looks to ATTICUS expecting an objection, but ATTICUS just gives a slight shake of his head. HECK takes a breath.) Asked her if he beat her up like that; she said, yes, he had. Asked her if he took advantage of her and she said, yes, he did. I went down to Robinson's house and brought him back. She identified him as the one, so I took him in. That's all there was to it.

MR. GILMER (returning to his seat at table. Thank you.

JUDGE TAYLOR. Any questions, Atticus? (ATTICUS turns his chair to the side and crosses his legs.)

ATTICUS (leaning back). Yes. Did you call a doctor, Sheriff?

HECK. No, sir.

ATTICUS (with slight edge). Why not?

HECK. It wasn't necessary, Mr. Finch. But she was mighty banged up.

ATTICUS. And you didn't----

JUDGE TAYLOR (cutting in). He's answered the question, Atticus.

ATTICUS (smiling). Just wanted to make sure, Judge. (Turns.) Sheriff, you say she was mighty banged up. In what way? Just describe her injuries, Heck.

HECK. There was already bruises comin' on her arms, and she had a black eye startin'.

ATTICUS. Which eye?

HECK. Let's see -- her left.

ATTICUS. Her left facing you, or her left looking the same way you were?

HECK (thinking about it). That'd make it her right. It was her right eye, Mr. Finch. I remember now, she was banged up on that side of her face. (ATTICUS looks at Tom, then back at HECK.)

ATTICUS (demanding). Please repeat what you said.

HECK. Her right eye.

ATTICUS. No -- you said she was banged up on that side of her face. Which side?

HECK. The right side. (REVEREND SYKES and HELEN are whispering.)

ATTICUS. That's all, Heck. (HECK steps down and walks over to bench.)

MR. GILMER (calling). Robert Ewell. (BOB EWELL hops up and comes up to the witness chair. If an extra is available to be Court Clerk, he administers the oath. Otherwise this can be done by Mr. Gilmer holding out the Bible and asking "Swear to tell the truth, the whole truth, and nothing but the truth?")

BOB EWELL (crowing). So help me God.

MR. GILMER (nods toward chair; EWELL sits). Mr. Robert Ewell?

BOB EWELL. That's m'name, cap'n.

MR. GILMER (doesn't particularly like EWELL). Are you the father of Mayella Ewell?

BOB EWELL. Well, if I ain't, I can't do anything about it now. Her ma's dead.

JUDGE TAYLOR (hard). Are you the father of Mayella Ewell?

BOB EWELL (cowed). Yes, sir.

JUDGE TAYLOR. Get this straight. There will be no audibly obscene speculations from anybody in this courtroom on any subject. Do you understand? (EWELL nods.) All right, Mr. Gilmer.

MR. GILMER. Thank you, sir. Mr. Ewell, tell us what happened on the evening of November twenty-first.

BOB EWELL. I was comin' in from the woods with a load o' kindlin' and just as I got to the fence, I heard Mayella screamin' like a stuck hog inside the house.

MR. GILMER. What time was it, Mr. Ewell?

BOB EWELL. Just 'fore sundown. Well, I was sayin', Mayella was screamin' like-- (The JUDGE clears his throat, irritated, and BOB EWELL hesitates.)

MR. GILMER (prodding). Yes? She was screaming?

BOB EWELL. She was raising this holy racket so I dropped m' load and run as fast as I could up to the window -- and I seen -- I seen---- (He gets up and points angrily at TOM ROBINSON.) I seen that black nigger yonder attackin' my Mayella! (There's a gasp from the spectators and a low moan from HELEN ROBINSON. MR. GILMER is going up to the bench, where he speaks quietly to the JUDGE. REVEREND SYKES leans across to JEM.)

REVEREND SYKES. Mr. Jem. Take Miss Jean Louise home. Mr. Jem, you hear me?

JEM (turning). Scout -- go home. Dill, you 'n' Scout go home.

SCOUT. You can't make me.

JEM (to REVEREND SYKES). I think it's okay, Reverend. She doesn't understand.

SCOUT. I most certainly do. I can understand anything you can.

REVEREND SYKES (disturbed). This ain't fit for Miss Jean Louise -- or you boys, either. (But REVEREND SYKES and the other spectators, talking excitedly to each other, are interrupted by JUDGE TAYLOR, who is banging his gavel for attention.)

JUDGE TAYLOR. Quiet! There has been a request that this courtroom be cleared of spectators, or at least of women and children -- a request that for the time being will be denied. People generally see what they look for, and hear what they listen for. And they have the right to make whatever decisions they consider best for their children. You may feel there's something here to be learned. Or you may decide you do not wish to face this problem. It's up to you to make the decision. I suggest you do it right now. I'm interrupting this trial for a ten minute recess. (The JUDGE bangs the gavel and rises. As he does, the curtain falls. If there's no curtain, the lights dim to black.)

END OF ACT ONE.

ACT TWO

THE HOUSELIGHTS DIM and the curtain, if used, is raised. If there is
no curtain, the stage lights come up.

Revealed is the trial scene with everyone back in place after the short
recess declared by JUDGE TAYLOR. BOB EWELL is in the witness
stand, MR. GILMER stands near him waiting, ATTICUS sits at his table
with TOM ROBINSON, and the spectators are seated, as before, on the
upper level.

JUDGE TAYLOR (looking about; dryly). I see we still have a few with
us. Well, let's get on. (He raps casually with his gavel and turns.) Mr.
Ewell, you will keep your testimony within the confines of Christian
English usage, if that's possible. (Nods.) Proceed, Mr. Gilmer.

MR. GILMER (uneasily). Where were we -- we were----

JUDGE TAYLOR (to the point). Mr. Ewell, did you see the defendant
attacking your daughter?

BOB EWELL. Yes, I did.

MR. GILMER (to JUDGE). Thank you, sir. (To EWELL.) You said you
were at the window?

BOB EWELL. Yes, sir.

MR. GILMER. Did you have a clear view of the room?

BOB EWELL. Yes, sir.

MR. GILMER. How did the room look?

BOB EWELL. All slung about, like there was a fight.

MR. GILMER. What did you do when you saw the defendant?

BOB EWELL. I run around the house to get in, but he run out the front door just ahead of me. I sawed who he was, but I was too distracted about Mayella to run after him. Mayella was in there squallin', so I run in the house.

MR. GILMER. Then what did you do?

BOB EWELL. I run for Heck Tate quick as I could. I knowed who it was all right, passed the house every day, lived down yonder in that nigger-nest. (Turns.) Jedge, I've asked this county for fifteen years to clean out that nest down yonder. They're dangerous to live around. (A put-upon citizen.) Sides devaluin' my property.

MR. GILMER (wincing; hurriedly). That's all. Thank you, Mr. Ewell. (Well satisfied with himself, EWELL hops down, smiling as he goes. He bumps into ATTICUS, who is approaching. There's a stir of amusement which EWELL construes as approval.)

ATTICUS (meanwhile; genially). Just a minute, sir. Could I ask you a question or two? (EWELL darts a glance at the JUDGE, who nods his head toward the witness chair.)

BOB EWELL (going back). Sure -- go ahead.

ATTICUS. Thank you, Mr. Ewell. Folks were doing a lot of running that night. Let's see, you say you ran to the house, you ran to the window, you ran inside, you ran for Mr. Tate. Did you, during all this running, run for a doctor?

BOB EWELL. Wadn't no need to.

ATTICUS. Didn't you think the nature of your daughter's injuries warranted immediate medical attention?

BOB EWELL. Never called a doctor in my life. If I had, would've cost me five dollars. That all the questions?

ATTICUS. Not quite. Mr. Ewell, you heard the sheriff's testimony, didn't you?

BOB EWELL (deciding it's safe to answer). Yes.

ATTICUS. Do you agree with his description of Mayella's injuries? Her right eye blackened, that she was beaten around the----

BOB EWELL. Yeah. I hold with everything Tate said.

ATTICUS. He said her right eye was blackened.

BOB EWELL. I holds with Tate.

ATTICUS. Mr. Ewell, can you read and write?

MR. GILMER. Objection. Can't see what witness's literacy has to do with the case, irrelevant 'n' immaterial.

ATTICUS (quickly). Judge, if you'll allow the question, plus another one, you'll soon see.

JUDGE TAYLOR. All right. But make sure we see, Atticus. (To GILMER.) Overruled.

ATTICUS (to EWELL). Will you write your name and show us?

BOB EWELL. I most positively will. How do you think I sign my relief checks? (There's an amused stir among the spectators. ATTICUS is taking envelope from his pocket and then unscrewing his fountain pen.)

SCOUT (during above; a worried whisper). Jem -- do you think Atticus knows what he's doin'?

JEM (uncertainly). Seems like he knows.

SCOUT. Far back as I c'n remember, he said never, never, never ask a question on cross examination unless you already know the answer.

JEM (he remembers, too).'Cause you might get an answer that'll wreck your case.

SCOUT (front again; nervously). Looks to me like he's gone frog-sticking without a light. (ATTICUS has presented the envelope to BOB EWELL, shaken the fountain pen and given that, too.)

ATTICUS. Would you write your name for us? Clearly now, so the jury can see you do it. (With a flourish, EWELL finishes writing his name.)

MR. GILMER (curiously). What's so interestin'?

JUDGE TAYLOR. He's left-handed.

ATTICUS (nodding). That's it.

BOB EWELL (outraged). What's my bein' lefthanded have to do with it? (To JUDGE.) He's tryin' to take advantage of me. Tricking lawyers like Atticus Finch take advantage of me all the time with their tricking ways. But it don't change what I saw, and I'll say it again -- I saw that nigger-

ATTICUS. That's all, Mr. Ewell. (The furious little man is stalking back to his seat.)

JEM (during above). I think we've got him.

SCOUT. Don't count your chickens.

DILL (hushed, eager). Her right eye was blacked so it had to be someone left-handed.

SCOUT (hushed in reply). Maybe Tom Robinson's left-handed.

MR. GILMER (calling). Mayella Violet Ewell.

(As MAYELLA approaches, the Court Clerk, if used, or otherwise MR. GILMER, administers the oath. "Swear to tell the truth, the whole truth and nothing but the truth.")

MAYELLA (nodding; softly). Yes. (She sits.)

MR. GILMER. Please tell the jury in your own words what happened on the evening of November twenty-first. (She doesn't reply.) Where were you at dusk on that evening?

MAYELLA. On the porch.

MR. GILMER (trying to prod her along). What were you doing on the porch?

JUDGE TAYLOR (as she hesitates). Just tell us what happened. You can do that, can't you? (As she doesn't reply.) What are you scared of? (She whispers something to him from behind her hand.) What was that?

MAYELLA (pointing at ATTICUS). Him. Don't want him doin' me like he done Papa, makin' him out left-handed.

JUDGE TAYLOR (perplexed). How old are you?

MAYELLA. Nineteen and a half.

JUDGE TAYLOR. I see. Well, Mr. Finch has no idea of scaring you, and if he did, I'm here to stop him. Now sit up straight and tell us what happened.

MAYELLA (taking a breath, and starting nervously). Well -- I was on the porch and -- and he came along and, you see, there was this old chiffarobe in the yard Papa'd brought in to chop up for kindlin'. Papa told me to do it while he was off in the woods, but I wasn't feelin' strong enough then, so he came by----

MR. GILMER. Who is "he"?

MAYELLA. That'n yonder. Robinson.

MR. GILMER. Then what happened?

MAYELLA. I said, come here, boy, and bust up this chiffarobe for me, I gotta nickel for you. So he came in the yard an' I went in the house to get him the nickel. An 'fore I knew it, he was at me. He got me 'round the neck. I fought, but he hit me agin and agin.

MR. GILMER (as she collects herself). Go on.

MAYELLA. An' he took advantage of me.

MR. GILMER. Did you scream and fight back?

MAYELLA. Kicked and hollered loud as I could.

MR. GILMER. Then what happened?

MAYELLA. Don't remember too good, but Papa came in the room and was hollerin' who done it? Then I sorta fainted, an' the next thing I knew Mr Tate was helpin' me over to the water bucket.

MR. GILMER. You fought Robinson hard as you could -- tooth and nail?

MAYELLA. I positively did.

MR. GILMER. But he took advantage of you?

MAYELLA (holding back a sob). I already told ya.

MR. GILMER. That's all for now. But stay here. I expect big, bad Mr. Finch has some questions.

JUDGE TAYLOR (primly). State will not prejudice the witness against counsel for the defense. (ATTICUS, smiling, has risen. He opens his coat, hooks his thumbs in his vest and without looking directly at MAYELLA, speaks casually to her.)

ATTICUS. Miss Mayella, I won't try to scare you for a while, not yet. Let's get acquainted. How old are you?

MAYELLA. Said I was nineteen, said it to the judge yonder.

ATTICUS. You'll have to bear with me, Miss Mayella. I can't remember as well as I used to. I might ask you things you've already said before, but you'll give me an answer, won't you? Good.

MAYELLA. Won't answer a word as long as you keep on mockin' me.

ATTICUS (startled). Ma'am?

MAYELLA. Long as you call me "ma'am" and say "Miss Mayella." (To JUDGE.) I don't have to take his sass.

JUDGE TAYLOR. That's just Mr. Finch's way. We've done business in this court for years and Mr. Finch is always courteous. Atticus, let's get on -- and let the record show that the witness has not been sassed.

ATTICUS. How many sisters and brothers have you?

MAYELLA. Seb'm.

ATTICUS. You the oldest?

MAYELLA. Yes.

ATTICUS. How long has your mother been dead?

MAYELLA. Don't know. Long time.

ATTICUS. How long did you go to school?

MAYELLA. Two year -- three year -- dunno.

ATTICUS. Miss Mayella, a nineteen-year-old girl must have friends. Who are your friends?

MAYELLA (puzzled). Friends?

ATTICUS. Don't you know anyone near your age? Boys -- girls -- just ordinary friends?

MAYELLA (angry). You makin' fun o' me again, Mr. Finch?

ATTICUS. Do you love your father, Miss Mayella?

MAYELLA. Love him, whatcha mean?

ATTICUS. Is he good to you, is he easy to get along with?

MAYELLA. He does tollable 'cept when----

ATTICUS. Except when?

MAYELLA. I said he does tollable.

ATTICUS (gently). Except when he's drinking? (The question is asked so gently that in spite of herself, MAYELLA nods.) When he's riled -- has he ever beaten you? (MAYELLA looks around, startled.)

JUDGE TAYLOR. Answer the question, Miss Mayella.

MAYELLA. My paw's never touched a hair o' my head---- (ATTICUS considers her a moment.)

ATTICUS. We've had a good visit, Miss Mayella. Now we'd better get to the case. You say you asked Tom Robinson to come chop up a -- what was it?

MAYELLA. A chiffarobe, a old dresser.

ATTICUS. Was Tom Robinson well known to you?

MAYELLA. Whaddya mean?

ATTICUS. Did you know who he was, where he lived?

MAYELLA (nodding). I knowed who he was. He passed the house every day.

ATTICUS (turning away; casually). Was this the first time you asked him to come inside the fence? (She jumps, looking about nervously.) Was this----

MAYELLA. Yes, it was.

ATTICUS. Didn't you ever ask him to come inside the fence before?

MAYELLA (ready now). I did not. I certainly did not.

ATTICUS (serenely). You never asked him to do odd jobs for you before?

MAYELLA (conceding). I mighta.

ATTICUS. Can you remember any other occasions?

MAYELLA. No.

ATTICUS (firmer). All right, now to what happened. You said Tom Robinson got you around the neck -- is that right?

MAYELLA. Yes.

ATTICUS. You say -- "he caught me and choked me and took advantage of me" -- is that right?

MAYELLA. That's what I said.

ATTICUS. Do you remember him beating you about the face? (She hesitates.) You're sure enough he choked you. All this time you were fighting back, remember? You kicked and hollered. Do you remember him beating you about the face? (She's looking about, uncertain how to reply.) It's an easy question, Miss Mayella, so I'll try again. Do you remember him beating you about the face?

MAYELLA. No, I don't recollect if he hit me. I mean, yes, I do, he hit me.

ATTICUS. Was your last sentence your answer?

MAYELLA. Yes, he hit -- I just don't remember -- it all happened so quick!

JUDGE TAYLOR. Don't you cry, young woman.

ATTICUS. Let her cry if she wants to, Judge. We've got all the time in the world.

MAYELLA (sniffing wrathfully). Get me up here an' mock me, will you? I'll answer any questions you got.

ATTICUS. That's fine. There's only a few more. Will you identify the man who attacked you?

MAYELLA. I will. That's him right yonder.

ATTICUS. Tom, stand up. Let Miss Mayella have a good look at you. Is this the man, Miss Mayella? (TOM stands. He is a powerful young man, but his left hand is curled up and held to his chest.)

JEM (hushed). Scout -- Reverend -- his left hand! He's crippled!

REVEREND SYKES (whispering). Caught in a cotton gin when he was a boy -- like to bled to death. Tore all the muscles loose.

ATTICUS. Is this the man who attacked you?

MAYELLA. It most certainly is.

ATTICUS (hard). How?

MAYELLA (raging). I don't know how, but he did. I said it all happened so fast I----

ATTICUS. Let's consider this calmly.

MR. GILMER. Objection. He's browbeating the witness.

JUDGE TAYLOR. Oh, sit down Horace.

ATTICUS. Miss Mayella, you've testified the defendant choked and beat you. You didn't say he sneaked up behind you and knocked you cold. Do you wish to reconsider any of your testimony?

MAYELLA. You want me to say something that didn't happen?

ATTICUS. No, ma'am, I want you to say something that did happen.

MAYELLA. I already told ya.

ATTICUS. He hit you? He blackened your left eye with his right fist?

MAYELLA (seeing the point). I ducked and it -- it glanced. That's what it did. I ducked and it glanced off.

ATTICUS. You're a strong girl. Why didn't you run?

MAYELLA. Tried to---

ATTICUS. And you were screaming all the time?

MAYELLA. I certainly was.

ATTICUS. Why didn't the other children hear you? Where were they? (No answer.) Why didn't your screams make them come running? (No answer.) Or didn't you scream until you saw your father in the window? You didn't scream till then, did you? (No answer.) Did you scream at your father instead of Tom Robinson? Is that it? (No answer.) Who beat you up? Tom Robinson or your father? (No answer.) Miss Mayella -- what did your father really see in that window? (She covers her mouth with her hands.) Why don't you tell the truth, child -- didn't Bob Ewell beat you up? (With this, ATTICUS turns away, and lets out a breath. He looks a little as though his stomach hurts. Mayella's face is a mixture of terror and fury.)

MAYELLA (gasping a quick breath and calling out). -- I got somethin' to say.

ATTICUS (walking back and sitting wearily at his table, with compassion). Do you want to tell us what happened?

MAYELLA. I got somethin' to say an' then I ain't gonna say no more. That black man yonder took advantage of me an' if you fine fancy gentlemen don't wanta do nothin' about it then you're all yellow stinkin' cowards, stinkin' cowards, the lot of you. Your fancy airs don't come to nothin' -- your ma'amin' and Miss Mayellarin' don't come to nothin', Mr. Finch. (She covers her face with her hands to hold back her sobs.)

MR. GILMER. That's all. (Helping her out of witness chair.) You can step down now. (As she continues on to bench to sit with her father, he turns to JUDGE.) Sir -- the State rests.

JUDGE TAYLOR. Shall we try to wind up this afternoon? How about it, Atticus?

ATTICUS. I think we can.

JUDGE TAYLOR. How many witnesses you got?

ATTICUS. One.

JUDGE TAYLOR. Well, call him.

ATTICUS (rising). I call Tom Robinson.

(TOM rises and walks toward the witness chair. Either the Court Clerk or MR. GILMER holds out the Bible to him. TOM can't put his crippled left hand on the Bible, so he touches it with his right.)

TOM. Sorry, sir.

JUDGE TAYLOR. That's all right, Tom. (TOM is asked, "Do you swear the evidence you're about to give is the truth, the whole truth, and nothing but the truth?")

TOM (nodding). I swear. (He is motioned into witness chair and he sits quiet and, naturally, afraid.)

ATTICUS. You're Tom Robinson, twenty-five years of age, married with three children, and you've been in trouble with the law once before. A thirty-day sentence for disorderly conduct. What did that consist of?

TOM. Got in a fight with another man. He tried to cut me. But it wasn't much. Not enough to hurt.

ATTICUS. You were both convicted?

TOM (nodding). I had to serve 'cause I couldn't pay the fine. The other fellow paid his'n.

ATTICUS. Were you acquainted with Mayella Violet Ewell?

TOM. Yes, sir. I had to pass her place goin' to and from the field every day.

ATTICUS. Whose field?

TOM. I work for Mr. Link Deas.

ATTICUS. You pass the Ewell place to get to work. Is there any other way to go?

TOM. No, sir, none's I know of.

ATTICUS. Tom, did she ever speak to you?

TOM. Why, yes, sir. I'd tip m' hat when I'd go by and one day she asked me to come inside the fence and bust up a chiffarobe.

ATTICUS. When did she ask you to chop up the -- the chiffarobe?

TOM. Mr. Finch, it was way last spring. After broke it up she said "I reckon I'll hafta give you a nickel, won't I" an' I said, "No, ma'am, there ain't no charge." Then I went home. That was way over a year ago.

ATTICUS. Did you ever go on the place again?

TOM. Yes, sir.

ATTICUS. When?

TOM. I went lots of times. (There's a murmur among the spectators, and JUDGE TAYLOR raps his gavel without comment.)

ATTICUS. Under what circumstances? (TOM doesn't quite understand.) Why did you go inside the fence lots of times?

TOM. She'd call me in. Seemed like every time I passed by yonder, she'd have somethin' for me to do -- choppin' kindlin', totin' water for her.

ATTICUS. Were you paid for your services?

TOM. No, sir, not after she offered me a nickel the first time. But I was glad to do it. Mr. Ewell didn't seem to help her none, and neither did the chillun, and I knowed she didn't have no nickels to spare.

ATTICUS. Where were the other children?

TOM. They were always around, all over the place.

ATTICUS. Would Miss Mayella talk to you?

TOM. Yes, sir, she talked to me.

ATTICUS. Did you ever -- at any time -- go on the Ewell property -- did you ever set foot on the Ewell property without an express invitation from one of them?

TOM. No, sir, Mr. Finch, I never did. I wouldn't do that, sir.

ATTICUS. Tom, what happened to you on the evening of November twenty-first? (The spectators draw in a collective breath and lean forward.)

TOM. Mr. Finch, I was goin' home as usual that evenin', and when I passed the Ewell place, Miss Mayella were on the porch, like she said she were. It seemed real quiet like, an' I didn't quite know why. She called to me to come there and help her a minute. Well, I went inside the fence an' looked for some kindlin' to work on, but I didn't see none, and she says "Naw, I got somethin' for you to do in the house. Th' old door's off its hinges." I said You got a screwdriver, Miss Mayella? She said she had. Well, I went up the steps and she motioned for me to come inside. (Takes a breath.) I went in an' looked at the door. I said Miss Mayella, this door look all right. Those hinges was all right. Then she shet the door. Mr. Finch, I was wonderin' why it was so quiet like, 'n it come to me that there weren't a chile on the place, not one of 'em, an' I said Miss Mayella, where the chillun? (TOM pauses to run his hand over his face.)

ATTICUS (quietly). Go on, Tom.

TOM. I say where the chillun, an' she says she was laughin' sort of -- she says they all gone to town to get ice creams. She says, "Took me a slap year to save seb'm nickels, but I done it. They all gone to town." (Intensely uncomfortable, shifting in his seat, TOM stops.)

ATTICUS. Tom, what did you say then?

TOM (taking a breath). I said somethin' like, why Miss Mayella, that's right smart o' you to treat 'em. An' she said "You think so?" I don't think she understood what I was thinkin' -- I meant it was smart of her to save like that, an' nice of her to treat 'em.

ATTICUS. I understand. Go on.

TOM. I said I best be goin', I couldn't do nothin' for her, an' she says oh yes I could, an' I ask her what, an' she says to just step on that chair yonder an' git that box down from on top of the chiffarobe.

ATTICUS. Not the same one you busted up?

TOM (smiling). No, sir, another one. Most as tall as the room. So I done what she told me, an' I was just reachin' when she -- she grabbed me round the legs, Mr. Finch. She scared me so bad I hopped down an' turned the chair over -- that was the only thing, only furniture 'sturbed in that room, Mr. Finch, when I left it. I swear 'fore God.

ATTICUS. What happened after you turned the chair over? (TOM has come to a stop, looking about the room nervously.) Tom, you've sworn to tell the whole truth. (TOM still hesitates. Prodding.) What happened after that?

JUDGE TAYLOR. Answer the question.

TOM. When I got down offa that chair, she sorta -- jumped at me.

ATTICUS. Jumped? Violently?

TOM. No, sir, she -- she hugged me. She hugged me round the waist. (There's a growing murmur as the spectators react to each other at this. It is cut short by Judge Taylor's gavel.)

ATTICUS. Tom -- what did she do then?

TOM (swallowing hard.) She says she never had her arms round a grown man before, an' she might as well start with me. She says "Hug me back." I say Miss Mayella lemme outa here an' I tried to run but she got her back to the door an' I'da had to push her. I didn't wanta harm her, Mr. Finch, an' I say lemme pass, but just when I say it Mr. Ewell yonder hollered through th' window.

ATTICUS. What did he say?

TOM. Somethin' not fittin' to say -- not fittin' for these folks 'n' chillun to hear.

ATTICUS. Tom, you must tell the jury what he said.

TOM. (shutting his eyes). He says you damn slut, I'll kill ya.

ATTICUS. Then what happened?

TOM (opening his eyes again; unhappily). I was runnin' so fast, Mr. Finch, I didn't know what happened.

ATTICUS. Tom, did you attack Mayella Ewell?

TOM. I did not, sir.

ATTICUS. Did you harm her in any way?

TOM. I did not.

ATTICUS. Did you resist her advances?

TOM. Mr. Finch, I tried to 'thout bein' ugly to her. I didn't wanta be ugly. I didn't wanta push her or nothin'.

ATTICUS. Let's go back to Mr. Ewell. Who was he talking to?

TOM. He were talkin' and lookin' at Miss Mayella.

ATTICUS. Then you ran.

TOM. I sure did.

ATTICUS. Why did you run?

TOM. I was scared, sir.

ATTICUS. Why were you scared?

TOM. Mr. Finch, if you was black like me, you'd be scared, too. (ATTICUS nods agreement with this, turns to MR. GILMER as though saying "Your witness," and starts back to his chair. MR. GILMER is rising and starting toward TOM. As this happens a VOICE calls in -- apparently from the spectators, but actually from offstage.)

VOICE. I want the whole lot of you know one thing right now. Tom Robinson's worked for me eight years an' I ain't had a speck o' trouble outa him. Not a speck.

JUDGE TAYLOR. (rapping angrily with his gavel). That's enough, Link Deas. If you have anything to say, you can say it under oath and at the proper time. (To jury.) You're to disregard the remark from Link Deas. (Turns.) Go ahead, Mr. Gilmer.

MR. GILMER. You were given thirty days for disorderly conduct, Robinson?

ATTICUS (from his chair). It was a misdemeanor and it's in the record, Judge.

JUDGE TAYLOR. Witness'll answer, though.

TOM. Yes, sir. I got thirty days. (MR. GILMER looks significantly at jury -- the audience -- then turns back to TOM.)

MR. GILMER. You're pretty good at busting up chiffarobes and kindling with one hand, aren't you?

TOM. Yes, sir. I reckon so.

MR. GILMER. Strong enough to choke the breath out of a woman.

TOM. I never done that, sir.

MR. GILMER. But you're strong enough?

TOM. I reckon so, sir.

MR. GILMER. Had your eye on her for a long time, hadn't you, boy?

TOM. No, sir. I never looked at her.

MR. GILMER. Then you were mighty polite to do all that chopping and hauling for her, weren't you, boy?

TOM. I was just tryin' to help out, sir.

MR. GILMER. That was mighty generous. Why were you so anxious to do that woman's chores?

TOM (hesitating). Looked like she didn't have nobody to help her.

MR. GILMER. With Mr. Ewell and seven children on the place, boy?

TOM. Well, I says it looked like they never help her none.

MR. GILMER. You did all this chopping from sheer goodness, boy?

TOM. Just tried to help her.

MR. GILMER. You're a mighty good fellow, it seems -- did all this for not one penny.

TOM. Yes, sir. I felt right sorry for her. She seemed to try more'n the rest of 'em.

MR. GILMER (he's got him). You felt sorry for her! You felt sorry for her! (The spectators are shifting uncomfortably at this. To the jury.) He felt sorry for her. (Turns back to TOM.) Now you went by the house as usual last November twenty-first and she asked you to come in and bust up the chiffarobe?

TOM. No, sir.

MR. GILMER. Do you deny you went by the house?

TOM. No, sir.

MR. GILMER. She says she asked you to bust up the chiffarobe. Is that right?

TOM. No, sir, it ain't.

MR. GILMER (his tone dangerous). You say she's lying, boy? (ATTICUS is rising to protest, but TOM handles the question.)

TOM. I don't say she's lying, Mr. Gilmer. I say she's mistaken in her mind. (ATTICUS sits again. The light on the court scene begins to dim except for a spot of light on SCOUT, JEM, and DILL who is increasingly upset.)

MR. GILMER (his tone rougher). Tell me, boy. Why did you run away?

TOM. I was scared, sir.

MR. GILMER. If you had a clear conscience, boy, why were you scared?

TOM. Like I says before, it weren't safe for any black man to be in a -- fix like that.

MR. GILMER (sarcastically). But you weren't in a fix. You testified you were resisting her advances. Were you scared she might hurt you -- a big fellow like you?

TOM. No, sir. I was scared I'd be in court, just like I am now.

MR. GILMER (his voice rising). Scared you'd have to face up to what you did?

TOM. No, sir. Scared I'd have to face up to what I didn't do.

MR. GILMER. You bein' impudent to me, boy?

TOM. I didn't go to be. (The light on the court scene has now dimmed, but a spot of light remains on the small group of spectators on the second level at R. DILL has been so upset, he isn't able to keep from crying. He's trying to disguise it, but JEM is aware.)

JEM. Scout -- go with Dill. Better take him outa here.

SCOUT. 'S the matter with him?

REVEREND SYKES. Might be a little thin-hided. I think you should go with him, Miss Jean Louise.

SCOUT (getting up, but resentful). Why me?

DILL (with an effort). I'm okay.

SCOUT (taking his hand). C'mon. (As they come down to DRC, the light behind them dims. As they go.) The heat got you? Ain't you feeling good?

DILL (getting himself in hand). Said I was okay.

SCOUT. Wanta see something? (As he nods, she takes something from her pocket.) Look at these.

DILL (examining them). Two little statues -- carved outa soap. Looks like a boy and a girl.

SCOUT. Got 'em from the knothole in the Radley tree.

DILL (looking from the little figures to SCOUT). Girl could be you.

Maybe the boy's Jem. Who carved 'em, you reckon?

SCOUT (shrugging). They was in the Radley tree.

(JEAN is coming on DR.)

DILL (considering). I think I'm beginning to understand why Boo Radley stays shut up in that house -- it's because he <u>wants</u> to stay inside.

SCOUT. That don't make any sense.

JEAN (speaking to SCOUT). Oh, yes, it does.

SCOUT (apparently not aware of JEAN, but reacting to what she said; conceding). Well, maybe.

DILL (agreeing with her last comment). Maybe he found out the way people can go outa their way to despise each other. (Almost a cry.) Why'd Mr. Gilmer have to do Tom Robinson that-away? Why'd he talk so hateful?

SCOUT. Dill, that's his job.

DILL. But he didn't have to sneer, and call him "boy. "

SCOUT. That's just Mr. Gilmer's way. They do all defendants that way, most lawyers, I mean.

DILL. Mr. Finch doesn't.

SCOUT. He's not an example, Dill, he's -- well, the same in the courtroom as he is at home -- or on the street. (DILL nods patiently, making SCOUT speak with a slight edge.) Might be better if Atticus was a little more -- if he was ----

DILL (exasperated). Don't you realize yet -- your father's not a run-of-the-mill man.

SCOUT (dubiously). Most people----

DILL (cutting in with a snort). Whatta you care about most people?

JEAN (smiling). You're expecting a lot from a very young girl, Dill.

DILL (not noticing JEAN; speaking to SCOUT). Maybe when you're older -- when you've seen more of the world -- this town even!

SCOUT (not liking Dill's superiority). If you've got over your cryin' fit, I guess I can take you back in.

DILL. Wasn't a cryin' fit. (Going with her.) Just didn't like the way Mr. Gilmer----

SCOUT (going to their seats; whispered superiority). That's because you don't understand about the law. (The light is coming up on the trial area with everyone seated except ATTICUS, who stands by his table.)

JEAN (thoughtfully, as the light is coming up). For an instant Scout and I were almost together. I expect there's a little of the older woman already in every young girl -- but they're not in touch very often. (Considering the trial.) We only seem to grow up at special times -- such as the time I walked back into that courthouse. (As JEAN steps off R, SCOUT punches JEM for attention.)

SCOUT. His speech to the jury? (JEM nods.) How long's he been at it?

JEM. Just finished going over the evidence. An' Scout -- we're gonna win! I don't see how we can't!

DILL (suspiciously). Did that Mr. Gilmer----

JEM. Nothin' new. Just the usual. Hush now. (ATTICUS, who has paused by the table, has been unbuttoning his vest, unbuttoning his collar, and loosening his tie.)

ATTICUS (looking up to the JUDGE). With the court's permission? (The JUDGE nods, and ATTICUS takes off his coat and vest and puts them on his chair.)

JEM (startled). Never saw him do that before.

SCOUT (equally impressed). Me either. (They are all leaning forward. ATTICUS looks directly out to the audience which is where the imaginary jury sits.)

ATTICUS (still upstage at his table). Gentlemen, this case is not a difficult one, it requires no minute sifting of complicated facts. This case is as simple as black and white. (He starts slowly front.) The State has not produced one iota of evidence that the crime Tom Robinson is charged with ever took place. It has relied instead upon the testimony of two witnesses -- witnesses whose testimony has not only been called into serious question on cross-examination, but has been flatly contradicted by the defendant. (Looks back at MAYELLA.) I have nothing but pity in my heart for the chief witness for the State. But my pity does not extend to her putting a man's life at stake. And this is what she's done -- done it in an effort to get rid of her guilt! I say guilt, because it was guilt that motivated her. She committed no crime, but she broke a rigid code of our society, a code so severe that whoever breaks it is hounded from our midst as unfit to live with. She's the victim of cruel poverty and ignorance, but she knew full well the enormity of her offense and she persisted in it. (He pauses and takes a breath.) She persisted and her subsequent reaction is something every child has done -- she tried to put the evidence of her offense away, out of sight. What was the evidence? Not a stolen toy to be hidden. The evidence that must be destroyed is Tom Robinson, a human being. Tom Robinson, a daily reminder of what she did. What did she do? She tempted a Negro. She did something that in our society is unspeakable. She's white and she tempted a Negro. Not an old uncle, but a strong, young black man. No code mattered to her before she broke it -- but it came crashing down on her afterwards! Her father saw what happened. And what did he do? (Looking at EWELL.) There is circumstantial evidence to the effect that Mayella Ewell was beaten savagely by someone who led almost exclusively with his left hand.

BOB EWELL (rising, fists clenched; furious). Damn you ta---- (JUDGE TAYLOR raps sharply for order, and HECK TATE motions EWELL down while ATTICUS watches, unimpressed.)

ATTICUS. Then Mr. Ewell swore out a warrant, no doubt signing it with his left hand, and Tom Robinson now sits before you, having taken the oath with the only good hand he possesses -- his right hand!

BOB EWELL (back on his feet; raging). You trickin' lyin----

JUDGE TAYLOR (rapping hard; angry). Shut your mouth, sir, or you'll be fined for contempt!

ATTICUS (as EWELL is forced back into his seat by HECK TATE). So a quiet, respectable Negro man who had the unmitigated temerity to feel sorry for a white woman is on trial for his life. He's had to put his word against his two white accusers. I need not remind you of their conduct here in court -- their cynical confidence that you gentlemen would go along with them on the assumption -- the evil assumption -- that all Negroes lie, that all Negroes are basically immoral, an assumption one associates with minds of their caliber. However, you know the truth -- and the truth is, some Negroes lie, and some Negro men are not to be trusted around women -- black or white. And so with some white men.

This is a truth that applies to the entire human race, and to no particular race. (He pauses to clean his glasses with his handkerchief, speaking in a casual lower key as he does.) In this year of grace, 1935, we're beginning to hear more and more references to Thomas Jefferson's phrase about all men being created equal. But we know that all men are not created equal -- in the sense that some men are smarter than others, some have more opportunity because they're born with it, some men make more money, some ladies make better cakes, some people are born gifted beyond the normal scope---- (He puts his glasses back on. Speaking directly to the audience he comes all the way down front. His manner has changed and he's speaking with controlled passion.) But there's one way in which all men are created equal. There's one human institution that makes the pauper the equal of a Rockefeller, the stupid man the equal of an Einstein. That institution, gentlemen, is a court of law. In our courts -- all men are created equal. (He looks out at the imaginary jury for a moment and then continues, totally committed.) I'm no idealist to believe so firmly in the integrity of our courts and in the jury system -- that's no ideal to me, it is a living, working reality. But a court is only as sound as its jury, and a jury is only as sound as the men who make it up. (Pauses to take a breath.) I'm confident that you gentlemen will review without passion the evidence you've heard, come to a decision, and restore this defendant to his family. In the name of God, do your duty! (ATTICUS continues to look front for a moment, then turns, walks back, and sits at the table with TOM ROBINSON. Nothing else happens on the stage until ATTICUS is seated. Then SCOUT reaches across and punches JEM.)

SCOUT. Did he say somethin' else? As he was walkin' back?

JEM. I think he said -- In the name of God, believe him!

DILL (tugging at both of them and pointing R). Looka yonder!

(CALPURNIA, carefully dressed, is coming shyly into the trial area from R. She pauses, waiting for recognition.)

JUDGE TAYLOR (becoming aware of her). It's Calpurnia, isn't it?

CALPURNIA. Yes, sir. Could I speak to Mr. Finch, please, sir? It hasn't got anything to do with -- with the trial.

JUDGE TAYLOR (nodding). Of course. (ATTICUS is crossing to her.)

ATTICUS (concerned). What is it, Cal? (She is whispering to him quickly, and he turns to the JUDGE.) Judge -- she says my children are missing, haven't turned up since noon. I -- could you----

MISS STEPHANIE CRAWFORD (calling). They're up here, Atticus (Nods to R.) Yonder.

ATTICUS (calling). Jem -- Scout -- come down. Meet me outside. (He crosses to the JUDGE whispers something. The JUDGE nods, and ATTICUS crosses R with CALPURNIA following. The light in the trial area dims. Meanwhile, JEM, SCOUT and DILL are coming down to DRC.)

SCOUT (to JEM). Is he mad?

JEM (shrugging). We'll find out. (ATTICUS, exhausted, is approaching them at DRC, followed by the outraged CALPURNIA. The light on the trial area is now quite dim, though there's still a little light on the patient spectators on the upper level.)

SCOUT (calling to him as he comes). Hey, Atticus.

Jem (excitedly). We've won, haven't we, Atticus?

ATTICUS (shortly). I've no idea. You've been here all afternoon? (They nod.) Well, go home with Calpurnia and stay home.

JEM. Aw, Atticus. Please let us hear the verdict.

ATTICUS. Have you done your reading today for Mrs. Dubose?

JEM. Not today. Please, sir. We----

ATTICUS. Tell you what -- you read to Mrs. Dubose, eat your supper, and then Cal can bring you back.

CALPURNIA (protesting). Sir?

ATTICUS. They've heard it all up to now! They might as well hear the rest.

DILL. Suppose the jury comes back before----

ATTICUS. Probably will. They might be out and back in a minute.

JEM. You think they'll acquit him that fast?

ATTICUS (quietly). Go do your reading, eat your supper, and if the jury is still out when you get back, you can wait up there with Cal and hear the verdict. (Deeply appreciative.) Thank you, Cal. (He turns and walks off into the darkness of the trial area.)

(JEAN is coming on DR and the remaining light on the stage is dimming off except for that on her.)

CALPURNIA (as the light on them is dimming; starting to herd them to R; indignantly). I should skin every one of you alive! The very idea ---- you children listening to all that! Mister Jem, don't you know better 'n to take your little sister to that trial? As for you, Mister Dill, you watch out your aunt doesn't ship you back to Meridian first thing in the mornin'! You oughta be perfectly ashamed of yourselves! (The light on them should have dimmed by now.)

JEAN. Calpurnia didn't stop expressing her outrage all the way home. When Jem ran over to read to Mrs. Dubose, Cal worked over Dill and me. (The light begins coming up again at DRC, revealing the same group, but they've now turned around and are heading back L, with CALPURNIA following.) And she was still upset as we finished supper and started back to the trial -- wondering what on earth we'd find.

CALPURNIA (her voice dropping as they get closer and go up onto upper level). Thought you was gettin' some kinda head on your shoulders, Mister Jem. Ain't you got any sense at all?

JEM. Don't you want to hear what happened?

CALPURNIA (an angry whisper as they go to their seats). Hush your mouth, sir. If Mr. Finch don't wear you out, I will!

DILL (looking front with glad surprise). The jury's still out!

Jem (looking about as he sits). Nobody's moved hardly. (The light on the trial area should not come up yet, but it will be at least partially visible from the spill of the light illuminating the spectators on the upper level. JUDGE TAYLOR is sitting where he was, his head on his hand, half asleep. MR. GILMER sits at his table going over some notes. MAYELLA still sits on her bench, but BOB EWELL isn't there. ATTICUS is also off as is HECK TATE and TOM ROBINSON. The spectators are all in place except MR. CUNNINGHAM.)

REVEREND SYKES (meanwhile; to JEM). They moved around some when the jury went out.

JEM. How long have they been out?

REVEREND SYKES. 'Bout an hour. Mr. Finch and Mr. Gilmer did some more talkin' and Judge Taylor charged the jury.

(MR. CUNNINGHAM is coming back to his seat on the upper level from L. He sits and whispers into NATHAN RADLEY's ear. He whispers to MISS STEPHANIE and she whispers to MISS MAUDIE. Meanwhile the conversation between REVEREND SYKES and JEM continues.)

DILL. How was he?

REVEREND SYKES. I'm not complainin' one bit. He was mighty fair-minded. I thought he was leanin' a little to our side. Made Mr. Ewell so mad, he stamped out of the room.

JEM. The judge isn't supposed to lean either way. 'Sides, we don't need it 'cause we won anyway. I don't see how any jury----

REVEREND SYKES (interrupting). Don't be so confident, Mister Jem. I've never seen any jury decide in favor of a black man over a white man.

JEM. This case is different. (Noticing.) What's all the whispering?

SCOUT (concerned). Must be somethin'.

(At this, BOB EWELL, very full of himself at this moment, walks on L, and crosses to sit with MAYELLA. He whispers to her, quite proud of himself. The trial area, however, is only partially lighted.)

DILL (uneasy). That Bob Ewell looks mighty pleased 'bout somethin'.

SCOUT (more concerned). Wonder where's Atticus. (There's no answer to this, and they look forward, waiting. Then JEAN speaks, and as she does, MISS MAUDIE leans across the space between them to whisper something to SCOUT.)

JEAN. We found out about the whispering. Atticus had been standing at the window at the end of the corridor outside and Bob Ewell came up to him, cursed him, told him he'd kill him if it took him the rest of his life, and when Atticus just stood there looking at him, Bob Ewell spat in his face. (SCOUT has turned, aghast, to whisper to JEM and DILL.)

According to what we heard, Atticus didn't bat an eye -- just took out a handkerchief and wiped his face.

(At this point, ATTICUS, pale but calm, his hands in his pockets, strolls on L, crosses to his table and sits. BOB EWELL nudges his daughter and gestures for her to look at ATTICUS. However he ignores them.)

SCOUT (whispering unhappily to JEM). How could he let Ewell get away with a thing like that?

JEM (just as unhappy). Dunno.

SCOUT (a hushed protest). But he's a dead shot----

DILL (defensively). That's not his way----

SCOUT (looking front). I'm gonna ask him about this.

JEAN. But his only comment -- all he said -- "I wish Bob Ewell wouldn't chew tobacco." (They are all waiting. She speaks quietly.) Several hours went by -- and we waited. I don't think anyone expected the jury to be out so terribly long.

SCOUT. Jem -- ain't it a long time?

JEM (pleased). Sure is, Scout.

JEAN. My brother thought it a favorable indication. Meanwhile, nobody moved about. Nobody left. (Takes a breath.) Then, suddenly it was happening!

(HECK TATE has come on L during this last, and he pauses there, his voice ringing with authority. Light is coming up fully now on the trial area.)

HECK. This court will come to order. (He steps back off L again.)

(JUDGE TAYLOR is rousing himself to sudden alertness, as is everyone else. HECK reappears L quickly, escorting TOM ROBINSON to the table where ATTICUS waits.)

HELEN (an involuntary call as her husband crosses). Tom---- (TOM looks up to her, then turns away quickly to sit beside ATTICUS.)

REVEREND SYKES (gently). Helen -- you promised.

HELEN (protesting). Reverend---- (But she stops herself. Agreeing in a low voice.) I promised.

JEM (looking out front, meanwhile; with growing dismay). Scout -- look. Look at the jury comin' in!

DILL (Jem's voice making him nervous; also looking front). What about 'em?

SCOUT (as she realizes; hushed). They're not looking at the defendant!

DILL (more nervous). What does it mean?

HECK (calling). The defendant will rise. (As TOM and ATTICUS are rising, HECK comes down front for an instant, turns and goes back to hand a slip of paper to JUDGE TAYLOR.)

DILL (during above business; a frantic whisper). What's it mean, Scout?

SCOUT (miserable). You're gonna see.

DILL. See what?

JEM. Hush. (JUDGE TAYLOR has read slip of paper. He suddenly seems very tired. He picks up his gavel, ready to rap with it, but sees it isn't necessary. He leans forward.)

JUDGE TAYLOR. The jury finds the defendant -- guilty. (There's a sigh from some, an intake of breath from others, and a low moan from HELEN. TOM turns to look up to her. The JUDGE is about to rap with his gavel, but decides against it again. Wearily, he tosses gavel on the table, leans back and nods to HECK.)

HELEN (not quite out loud, her lips forming his name). Tom -- Tom---- (ATTICUS has put a hand on Tom's shoulder and is speaking earnestly into his ear as HECK TATE approaches. ATTICUS then steps aside and HECK escorts TOM off L with him. BOB EWELL, muttering disdainfully past the JUDGE, goes off L followed by MAYELLA. MR. GILMER also goes off L, as does JUDGE TAYLOR. The reactions below are expressed during this and follow as quickly as the verdict registers.)

SCOUT (in shock). We lost! It's all lost!

JEM (heartbroken). How could they find him guilty?

CALPURNIA (an unhappy protest voiced mainly to herself). Not right you children should see such things! Not right any children should see such things!

DILL (hushed). What happens now? What can we do?

JEM (bitterly). If the evidence don't matter, I don't see there's anything----

DILL (whispered horror). But they're not going to hurt Tom Robinson? Your father'll do something. Mr. Finch won't let' em. He'll -- he---- (He's stopped by REVEREND SYKES' hand on his shoulder, and as he looks back, he sees that the REVEREND, HELEN and CALPURNIA are standing respectfully. He realizes, and rises to his feet as does Jem. During the above, ATTICUS has been left alone in the trial area. He's put some papers in his brief case, slung his coat over his shoulder, and, utterly exhausted, he's collecting himself, unaware of those on the second level.)

SCOUT (continuing meanwhile, her fists clenched, and leaning forward). They c'n spit in his face, and find Tom Robinson guilty! But no matter what any of 'em says -- Atticus -- he's----

REVEREND SYKES (his hand on her shoulder now). Miss Jean Louise---- (Interrupted, SCOUT turns to see them standing. Across the space to the left, MISS MAUDIE ATKINSON is also standing to show her respect. The other white spectators who have started off L carrying their chairs pause now, possibly out of curiosity, but they're also standing. ATTICUS takes a breath, and starts R.) Miss Jean Louise -- stand up. Stand up -- your father's passing. (SCOUT gets to her feet with the others as her father continues R, going off down R past the impassive JEAN. As this is happening, the lights dim off everywhere except on JEAN. REVEREND SYKES helps HELEN off L while the others take off the set pieces used for the trial scene. While that part of the stage is in darkness, the curtains used for the trial are taken away, and the set, while not yet lighted, is as it was earlier in the play. As this is happening, JEAN is speaking, beginning as ATTICUS completes his exit R.)

JEAN (looking after her father). When we spoke to Atticus later, Jem started to cry. He wanted to know how the jury could do it. (She turns front.) I'd never seen my father so close to bitter. "I don't know how," he told us, "but they did it. They've done it before, and they did it today and they'll do it again. And when they do it -- seems only children weep." (She takes a breath.) As for Bob Ewell, he walked out of the courtroom expecting to find himself the town hero, but it turned out only a few really believed him -- Atticus had destroyed his last shred of credibility. All Ewell got for his pain was -- was, okay, we convicted the Negro, but now you -- you get back to your dump. Ewell started making terrible threats. This time we should have believed him. This time he was telling the truth.

(SCOUT has come on L, crossed to DC, and then looks about.)

JEAN. I hurried home ahead of Jem and Dill. I didn't want them to see me going back to the knothole in the tree. I'd put a note there thanking whoever it was who left me the nice surprises. (SCOUT is crossing quickly to the tree, and reaching up.) I thought there might be an answer. What I found----

SCOUT (as she touches it; with dismay). Cement! Someone filled it with cement!

(NATHAN RADLEY is strolling on L, not yet seen by SCOUT.)

NATHAN (to her back, dryly). Anything the matter?

SCOUT (startled, whirling around). What? (Collecting herself.) No -- nothing the matter. (Half a question.) There's cement in the knothole. (JEAN goes off R.)

NATHAN (nodding). I filled it up.

SCOUT (it takes courage to ask). Why'd you do that, sir?

NATHAN. Tree's dying. You plug' em with cement when they're sick. (Going toward his house.) You ought to know that, Miss Jean Louise.

SCOUT (after him). The tree don't look sick to me. (But he continues on into the house, shutting the door.)

(JEM and DILL are coming on L.)

SCOUT (muttering to herself). Whoever carved the soap statues, it wasn't him.

JEM (to SCOUT). Why'd you run ahead? Scared of old Mr. Ewell?
SCOUT. Not one bit.
JEM. Why should he stand outside the courthouse talkin' so mean? His side won.

(MISS STEPHANIE CRAWFORD is coming on L.)

DILL (too much to bear). But he hasn't won really. We can still do something?
JEM (bitterly). Looks to me like the minute Mayella Ewell opened her mouth and screamed, Tom Robinson was a dead man!
DILL (shocked protest). Jem!
MISS STEPHANIE (bustling over). I'm absolutely surprised at you children. Did Atticus give you permission to go to court?

(JEM shrugs in reply. MISS MAUDIE ATKINSON is coming on L.)

MISS STEPHANIE. Why were you sitting over in the colored balcony? Several people mentioned it. Wasn't it right close over there?
MISS MAUDIE (disgusted). Hush, Stephanie.
MISS STEPHANIE (turning). Do you think it's wise for children to----
MISS MAUDIE (interrupting). We've made the town this way for them. They might as well learn to cope with it.
MISS STEPHANIE. Least they don't have to wallow in it.
MISS MAUDIE (tartly). What happened in court is as much a part of Maycomb as missionary teas.
MISS STEPHANIE (starting up onto her porch). Well -- excuse me. Don't suppose they understood anyway. (Pauses before going in. With what may be genuine sympathy.) Too bad you had to see your daddy get beat. (With this, she goes in. JEM and SCOUT are hurt by her comment, as is DILL.)
DILL (beginning softly). When I get grown, I think I'll be a clown.
JEM (not quite focusing). What, Dill?
DILL. Yes, sir, a clown. There ain't one thing in this world I can do about folks, so I'm gonna join the circus and laugh my head off.

JEM. You've got it backwards, Dill. Clowns are sad. It's folks that laugh at them.

DILL. I'm gonna be a new kind of clown. I'm gonna stand in the middle of the ring and laugh -- laugh in their faces! (MISS MAUDIE has been watching, disturbed by their unhappiness.)

MISS MAUDIE. Don't pay attention to what she says about Atticus.

JEM. What do you mean?

MISS MAUDIE. I simply would like you to know that there are some men in this world who were born to do our unpleasant jobs for us. Your father's one of them.

JEM. Oh -- well----

MISS MAUDIE. Don't you "oh well" me, sir. You're just not old enough to appreciate what I said.

JEM (troubled). I always thought Maycomb folks were the best folks in the world.

MISS MAUDIE. We're the safest folks in the world. We're so rarely called on to be Christians, but when we are, we've got men like Atticus to go for us.

JEM. Who feels that way 'sides you?

MISS MAUDIE. The handful of people in this town who say that fair play isn't marked "White only."

JEM (must know). But who? Who did one thing to help Tom Robinson?

MISS MAUDIE. His friends, for one thing, and people like us. We exist, too. People like Judge Taylor. People like Heck Tate. Start using your head, Jem. Did it ever strike you that Judge Taylor naming Atticus to defend Tom was no accident? That Judge Taylor might have had his reasons?

SCOUT. S'right, Jem. Usually the court appoints some new lawyer -- one who is just startin'.

MISS MAUDIE. You're beginning to realize! A little more to it than you thought! (Pressing.) Whether Maycomb knows it or not, we're paying your father the highest tribute we can pay a man. We trust him to do right.

SCOUT. Then why did he get beat?

MISS MAUDIE (snorting). Miss Stephanie talks nonsense. Maybe he didn't get an acquittal, but he got something. I was sitting in court waiting, and as I waited, I thought -- Atticus Finch won't win, he can't win, but he's the only man in these parts who can keep a jury out so long in a case like this. And I thought to myself, take note of this time and this place. It's 1935 and it's Maycomb, Alabama, and we're making a step -- it's just a baby-step, but it's a step. (They are looking at her thinking about what she's just said. She takes a breath and collects herself.) I'm going into my kitchen now, and I'm going to make a cake. And I'd be pleased if you'd all come over later and have some of my cake.

SCOUT (subdued). Yes, Miss Maudie.

JEM. Thank you.

MISS MAUDIE. Mister Dill?

DILL (half jumping). Yes -- I'll come. Thank you. (With this MISS MAUDIE goes up and enters her house.) I better stop over to Aunt Rachel. (Pauses. Considering.) They trust him to do right. (But this is too much for right now. He'll think about it some other time. Suddenly brightening.) I'll be back -- and then we'll all have cake. (With this, DILL runs off L. SCOUT takes Jem's hand and they go into the house.)

(As SCOUT and JEM are going, JEAN comes back on DR.)

JEAN. Tom Robinson was taken to the Enfield Prison Farm, about seventy miles away. Atticus thought Tom had a good chance for a new trial, but Tom just couldn't hope any more. His old employer made a job for Helen so she could support the children, but she had to pass the Ewell place and they shouted and chucked things at her. She was terrified till Heck Tate went out and made them desist. Then Ewell's threats got worse. Partly he blamed Judge Taylor, but the main focus of his sick fury was Atticus. The only man in Maycomb ever to be fired from the WPA for laziness was Ewell, and somehow he twisted that onto Atticus, too -- said Atticus had got his job. It looked to us that it was building to a blow-up, but Atticus just went about his business -- working on Tom's appeal. Then suddenly death was among us.

(JEM has come out of the house as CALPURNIA is coming out of Mrs.

Dubose's house, and they meet in the yard.)

JEAN. First it was Mrs. Dubose. Jem had started over to read to her, when he was stopped by Cal, who'd gone over to lend a hand. The doctor had just told her that Mrs. Dubose had passed away.

(SCOUT and ATTICUS are coming onto the porch, looking at CAL and JEM, who are approaching.)

JEAN. And Jem found out why he'd been reading to her. She'd been given morphine for her pain, and she'd become an addict -- but she wanted to break herself of it before she died. She wanted to leave the world beholden to nobody and nothing. Jem's reading was a distraction. It was a help.

JEM (looking up to ATTICUS). That's why you said I had to read to her?

(BOB EWELL, whittling a piece of wood with a knife, is coming on the upper level L and starting slowly R. He's full of a private joke that gives him a momentary sense of superiority.)

ATTICUS (nodding). Her views on a lot of things were quite different from mine, but I was glad she asked you to read to her because I wanted you to see----

BOB EWELL (cutting in). Hello, Finch.

ATTICUS (looking at him, then turning back to JEM, continuing). I wanted you to see what real courage is.

BOB EWELL (gloating). Got some good news, Finch.

ATTICUS (glancing at EWELL). Courage isn't a man with a knife in his hand. Jem -- it's when you know you're licked before you begin, but you begin anyway and you see it through no matter what. You rarely win -- but sometimes you do. Mrs. Dubose won, all ninety-eight pounds of her!

BOB EWELL. Don't'cha wanta hear, Finch?

(HELEN ROBINSON, distraught, hurries on DR.)

HELEN. Mr. Finch -- Cal -- please----

ATTICUS (coming down off porch). What is it? What's wrong, Helen?

(HECK TATE is coming on DL, crossing quickly.)

HECK (calling). Atticus----

ATTICUS. Cal----

CALPURNIA (putting an arm around HELEN; anxiously). One of the children?

HELEN (can hardly talk). It's not the children----

ATTICUS (to HECK). What is it?

BOB EWELL (getting back at them). I'll tell you -- they shot that nigger!

HECK (ignoring EWELL). Tom's dead!

HELEN. Mr. Finch -- they shot Tom!

ATTICUS. Heck?

HECK (nodding). He was running. It was during their exercise period. They said he just broke into a blind raving charge at the fence and started climbing over -- right in front of them.

ATTICUS. Oh, my God! (Turns.) Cal, please, take Helen inside. You children go inside.

BOB EWELL. They put seventeen bullet holes in him.

ATTICUS (to his numb children). I said for you to go inside. (Turning to HECK, not seeing that they aren't moving.) Didn't they try to stop him? Didn't they give him any warning?

HECK (nodding). They shouted, and then they fired a few shots in the air. They didn't shoot at him till he was almost over the fence.

HELEN. Mr. Finch -- how could they shoot Tom?

ATTICUS (with difficulty). Helen -- to them he was just an escaping prisoner. He wasn't Tom to them.

HELEN (bewildered). Why didn't he wait for the appeal?

ATTICUS. I don't know. I told him we had a chance, but I couldn't say we had more than a chance. I guess Tom was fed up with white men's chances.

BOB EWELL. Ain't it just like a nigger to cut 'n' run?

CALPURNIA (firmly). You come inside, Helen.

ATTICUS (turning to address BOB EWELL directly, barely able to control his anger). Do you have anything more you want to say, Mr. Ewell?

BOB EWELL (starting to go, then stopping, overwhelmed with spite). Yes -- I say there's one down -- (With his knife, he slashes a piece from his whittling.) -- two to go! Now guess who's gonna be next! (He slashes another piece from his whittling and walks off L.)

HECK (thoughtfully). I think I'd keep the shotgun loaded with double O.

JEM (from the porch). He doesn't have a shotgun.

ATTICUS. I can't believe Bob Ewell would ever really come after me. But if he should, I'll deal with him.

HECK (considering). I expect you would.

ATTICUS (dropping his voice). Was Tom really shot up that much?

HECK (unhappily). There's talk, but I don't know. (Going L.) You better be careful, Atticus.

ATTICUS (after him). Sure -- thanks, Heck.

JEM (firmly). Atticus, I'm worried about you. And I think you should get a gun.

ATTICUS. I told you twice to go inside. Let's all go and be with Helen. (As they're starting in. Pointedly.) And remember -- she's someone who's heard enough about guns. (As they go into the house, the light begins to dim except for a small isolated bit of illumination on JEAN at extreme DR. As she speaks, the light continues to dim until the stage is entirely dark except on her, and she's only dimly seen.)

JEAN. Atticus was underestimating what anger and sick frustration could do to an already unbalanced man. The night we found out -- there was a pageant at the school auditorium and Jem said he'd take me. It was to be our longest journey together. Wind was coming up and Jem said it might be raining before we got home. Heavy clouds had blacked out the moon, and it was pitch dark. Before we left, Cal had a pinprick of apprehension. When I asked what was the matter, she said "Somebody just walked over my grave." On the way to school, Jem had a flashlight. (At this, JEM at LC turns on a pinpoint flashlight, directing it into Scout's face.)

JEM (teasing). You scared? Scared of haints?

SCOUT (scornfully). Haints, hot steams, incantations, secret signs -- I'm too old.

JEM (reciting). "Angel bright, life-in-death, get off the road, don't suck my breath."

SCOUT (sharply). Cut it out!

JEM. You're scared now because we're passin' Boo Radley's place.

SCOUT. I'm not scared. 'Sides, he must not be home.

JEM. How c'n ya tell?

SCOUT (logically). If he was, there wouldn't be a bird singing in the Radley tree. Hear that mocker? (As they listen to the understated bird-song, the flashlight goes out.) Turn on your light again.

JEM. Somethin' wrong with it. C'mon. Gimme your hand.

SCOUT (as they're going). How do you know where we're at?

JEM. I can tell we're under the tree now because we're passing through a cool spot. (As they're going off L.) Careful.

JEAN. The trip back from the pageant was more eventful. The moon had been in and out of the heavy rainclouds, but as we started home it was black dark -- and there was the stillness that sometimes comes before a thunderstorm. (Her voice increasingly involved.) Jem thought he heard something, and we stopped to listen. Then we walked a few more steps, and he stopped again. I thought he was trying to scare me, but that wasn't it. He held my hand tight and pulled me along fast. Then we stopped suddenly. (There are sounds of several steps being taken, off L, and then they stop.) I thought I heard steps following, too. (There's a rumble of distant thunder. SCOUT speaks to JEM, in the darkness at extreme L. The light on JEAN has dimmed off. The stage is in total darkness.)

SCOUT (voice in the darkness). Jem, are you afraid?

JEM (voice). Think we're not too far to the tree now.

SCOUT. Reckon we ought to sing, Jem?

JEM (worried). No. Be real quiet, Scout. (There's another rumble of thunder.)

SCOUT. Just the thunderstorm gettin' closer.

JEM (more worried). No, not that -- Listen! (From off L there's the sound of someone running [understated] toward them.)

SCOUT (with sudden alarm). I hear! Jem!

JEM (a shout; imperative). He's coming! Run, Scout! Run! Run!

SCOUT (in trouble). I tripped! Jem -- help me!

JEM (frantic). Where are ya? Scout -- C'mon!

SCOUT (growing panic). Can't see! I don't know where----

JEM. Get away, Scout -- Run! (Then JEM cries out as apparently someone grabs him. There's a sound of struggling. A man's voice is heard -- angry, unintelligible.)

MAN. Got cha -- now you'll -- damn ya -- show 'em---- (There's a crack and JEM screams with pain.)

SCOUT (hushed terror). Jem! (Then a cry.) Help us -- someone -- help. (The blackness is split as the Radley door is suddenly swung wide open, the light from inside silhouetting a big MAN in the doorway. There may be a clap of thunder accompanying this action. The light may briefly reveal a man standing over JEM on the ground, and struggling with the stricken SCOUT. The less seen the better. The light is quickly cut off as the MAN slams the door behind him and joins the struggle in the darkness DL. There's a moment of continued struggle, grunts, Scout's sobs, and then a man's cry of pain. "Ahhhh!")

(The sounds of struggle stop. JEM is picked up by the MAN and carried R to the Finch house, where the porch light is turned on, and ATTICUS comes out. [Note: If the man can't carry Jem, he should be supporting, with Jem's arm over his shoulder. In either case, Jem's downstage arm is hanging as though broken.] SCOUT, who has been flung to the ground, is watching from there. The attacker isn't visible.)

ATTICUS (as he comes out). Who called? What is it? Who-- (Stops himself as he sees MAN approaching with JEM. He goes off porch to help.) Oh, my God -- Jem! (Helping MAN up with him. Calling ahead.) Cal -- telephone Doctor Reynolds quick! Tell him urgent! (As MAN is taking JEM inside.) Put him down on---- (Turns.) Scout -- where's Scout!

SCOUT (struggling up). I'm here! (He's rushing to her.) I'm all right -- the man's gone. But he did somethin' awful to Jem. Atticus -- is Jem dead?

ATTICUS (taking her back to porch). He's unconscious. Looks like his arm's broken.

(CALPURNIA is out onto porch.)

CALPURNIA. Scout all right?

ATTICUS. Yes.

CALPURNIA. Miss Eula May's getting Doctor Reynolds.

SCOUT (needing reassurance). Jem's not dead, is he, Cal?

CALPURNIA. Passed out from the pain. Who did this? Who would----

ATTICUS (going in with SCOUT). Call Heck Tate, please. Tell him someone's been after my children. (As ATTICUS goes in, CALPURNIA turns to stare into the night, involuntarily clenching her fists with outrage. But she's part of a "lawing family" and she's needed inside. She hurries back in. The light has revealed JEAN again at DR.)

JEAN. After ten forevers, Doctor Reynolds finished with Jem. He said it looked like someone tried to wring his arm off, and it would be a while before Jem could play football again. He added his assurance that Jem wasn't dead -- only under sedation.

(A man with a flashlight, HECK TATE, has come on L and is approaching the porch.)

JEAN. Meanwhile Heck Tate had been investigating and when he came to the porch, there was something odd about him.

HECK (calling). Atticus----

(ATTICUS comes out on the porch.)

ATTICUS. Come in, Heck. Did you find anything? (Incredulous.) I can't conceive anyone who'd do this.

HECK. Let's stay outside.

(SCOUT is coming onto porch as ATTICUS steps down to HECK.)

ATTICUS (puzzled). What is it, Heck?

HECK. Bob Ewell's lyin' on the ground yonder with a kitchen knife stuck up under his ribs. He's dead, Mr. Finch.

(ATTICUS is stunned, and SCOUT gulps. The MAN comes out of the house, standing quietly watching from back by the glider.)

ATTICUS (bleakly). Dead? Are you sure?

HECK. Good and dead. He won't hurt these children again.

ATTICUS. But----

HECK (his anger getting the better of him). The mean-as-hell, low-down skunk with enough liquor in him to make him brave enough to kill children!

ATTICUS (in shock). I thought he'd got it out of him the day he spat at me. And if he hadn't, thought I was the one he'd come after.

HECK. Now you know better. (To SCOUT.) He broke Jem's arm, and he grabbed you. Then what happened?

SCOUT. Someone came out from -- to help. Someone----

HECK. Who was it?

SCOUT (coming aware of him). Well, there he is, Mr. Tate -- he'll tell you his name. (They all turn to look at the MAN at the back of the porch. He's pale, nervous, withdrawn. As SCOUT looks at him, she begins to realize; she takes a step toward him. Gently.) Hey -- Boo.

ATTICUS (to SCOUT). His right name's Mr. Arthur -- Boo is just a nickname. Jean Louise, this is Mr. Arthur Radley. Maybe you'd like to take him in. You can sit by Jem.

SCOUT. Like to come in, Mr. Boo? (He nods, takes her arm and they go in.)

ATTICUS (turning). Well, Heck -- I guess the thing to do -- Jem's a minor, of course. It'll come before county court.

HECK. What will, Mr. Finch?

ATTICUS. Of course it's clear-cut self-defense.

HECK. Mr. Finch, do you think Jem killed Bob Ewell?

ATTICUS. They were struggling in the dark. He probably got hold of Ewell's knife.

HECK. It wasn't Jem.

ATTICUS. That's kind of you, and I know you're doing it from the good of your heart. But I won't have him grow up with a whisper about him. I won't hush up----

HECK (sharply). Hush up what? Jem didn't do it.

ATTICUS. Then who ----

HECK (flatly). I'll tell you -- Bob Ewell fell on his knife. He killed himself.

ATTICUS. Heck, I won't have my children hear me say something different from what they know to be true. If I do, I won't have them any more. I can't live one way in town and another way in my home.

HECK. Mr. Finch, I hate to fight you when you're like this. You've been under a strain no man should ever have to go through. Maybe that's why you're not putting two and two together.

ATTICUS (trying to understand). If it wasn't Jem----

HECK. Of course it wasn't. His arm was broken.

ATTICUS (looking toward porch). Then it was -- it would have to be----

HECK (emphatically). Put that thought outa your mind, Mr. Finch. I already told you what happened.

(SCOUT is coming back onto the porch.)

ATTICUS. But if it was----

HECK. This isn't your decision, Mr. Finch, it's all mine. It's my decision, and my responsibility. And there's not much you can do about it.

ATTICUS. What are you saying, Heck?

HECK. I'm saying there's a black man dead for no reason, and the white man responsible for it is dead. So let the dead bury the dead, this time, Mr. Finch.

ATTICUS. What about----

HECK. I never heard tell it's against the law for a citizen to do his utmost to prevent a crime from being committed, which is exactly what Boo Radley did. Now maybe you'll say it's my duty to tell the town all about it and not hush it up. Know what'd happen then? All the ladies in Maycomb, including my wife, would be knocking on his door bringing angel food cakes. To my way of thinking, dragging him with his shy ways into the limelight -- that's a sin. (He starts L, then pauses.) I may not be much, Mr. Finch, but I'm still sheriff of Maycomb County, and Bob Ewell fell on his knife. (Going.) Good night, sir. (ATTICUS turns and is surprised to see SCOUT.)

ATTICUS. Scout.

SCOUT. Yes, Atticus?

ATTICUS. Mr. Ewell fell on his knife. Can you possibly understand?

SCOUT. Sir -- it looks to me -- what Heck said----

(But she's interrupted by BOO, who has come back onto the porch.)

BOO. Jean Louise?

SCOUT. Yes, Mr. Boo?

BOO. Will you take me home? (She nods, offers her arm, and they start for the Radley house. It's getting much brighter.)

ATTICUS (after them). Arthur---- (They pause.) Thank you for my children, Arthur. (Then SCOUT and BOO continue toward the Radley house.)

JEAN (quietly). I remember -- the moon had come out -- the storm had passed over -- and I was being escorted by Boo Radley. (They've gone up onto the Radley porch. BOO nods, and goes inside.) He went inside and I never saw him again. But when I turned around, standing on Boo's porch -- I saw something else. (SCOUT pauses there, looking off.) A young boy and girl shouting, running to meet their father coming home, the boy going after Mrs. Dubose's camellias, the children excited about surprises found in the knothole -- and then a stormy night, and those children need him! (JEAN turns toward her father who is waiting for SCOUT.) Atticus -- I was already beginning to stand in other people's shoes! The thing you wanted, Atticus -- (He doesn't hear. SCOUT is running back to him ruefully.) But -- did you ever know?

SCOUT (running up). Atticus -- what Heck Tate said about Boo -- about dragging him into the limelight -- Heck was right.

ATTICUS. What do you mean?

SCOUT. I mean, it'd be sort of like shooting a mockingbird, wouldn't it?

ATTICUS (quietly happy). Yes -- yes, it would. Let's go in and sit with Jem.

JEAN (softly, her lips just forming the words). You did know.

SCOUT (as they're going). All those ideas we had about Boo Radley -- But, Atticus -- he's real nice. (The curtain, if used, is falling. Otherwise the lights are dimming off.)

ATTICUS (affectionately, as they're going in). Most people are, Scout -- when you finally see them.

END OF PLAY

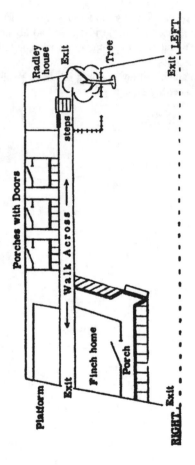

Platform

Exit

Finch home

Porch

Walk Across →

← Walk Across

Porches with Doors

steps

Radley house

Exit

Tree

RIGHT Exit

Exit LEFT

To Kill a Mockingbird

NOTES ABOUT CHARACTERS

GENERAL NOTE ABOUT ALL CHARACTERS.

Everyone in this play lives in southern Alabama and accordingly might be expected to speak with a Southern accent. It would be a disservice to the play, however, if the audience starts admiring the accent rather than listening to the content of the lines. The playwright strongly urges that the actors understate any attempt at a regional accent rather than risk overstating it -- thus calling attention to it and hurting the flow of the play. An authentic pattern of Southern speech is already contained in the lines, and this is sufficient.

SCOUT: A young girl about to experience the events that will shape the rest of her life, she should, ideally, seem as young as nine. She has such an important role to play, however, that it will probably be necessary to cast an older girl in the part. Scout is courageous and forthright. If a question occurs to her, she'll ask it.

JEAN LOUISE: She's Scout, grown older, looking back on the time she was the young Scout, looking for answers to questions that still exist in her memory of that time. She isn't connected directly to the people in the play, though on occasion there's almost a communication between them. What is happening on stage is Jean Louise re-living the dramatic time of her youth in her mind. There should be a subtle suggestion about her appearance and manner that suggests Scout grown-older.

JEM: He is a few years older than his sister Scout, and like his sister -- perhaps even more than his sister -- he's reaching out to understand their unusual and thus not conventionally-admirable father. Probably the strongest undercurrent in Jem is his desire to communicate with his father.

ATTICUS: He's tall, quietly impressive, reserved, civilized and nearly fifty. He wears glasses and because of the poor sight in his left eye, looks with his right eye when he wants to see something well. It's typical of Atticus that when he found out he was an extraordinary shot with a rifle, he gave up shooting -- because he considered it gave him an unfair advantage over the animals. He's quietly courageous and without heroics, he does what he considers just. As someone comments about him -- "We trust him to do right."

CALPURNIA: Black, proud and capable, she has raised the motherless Scout and Jem. She's a self-educated woman and she's made quite a good job of it. Her standards are high and her discipline as applied to Scout and Jem is uncompromising.

DILL: Small, blond and wise beyond his years, he is about the same age as Jem. Dill is neater and better dressed than his friends. There's an undercurrent of sophistication to him, but his laugh is sudden and happy. Obviously there is a lack in his own home life, and he senses something in Atticus that's missing from his own family relationship.

MAUDIE ATKINSON: Younger than Atticus, but of his generation, she's a lovely sensitive woman. Though belonging to the time and place of this play, she has a wisdom and compassion that suggests the best instincts of the South of that period.

WALTER CUNNINGHAM: Cunningham is a hard-up farmer who shares the prejudices of this time and place but who is nevertheless a man who can be reached as a human being. He also has seeds of leadership, for when his attitude is changed during the confrontation with Atticus, he takes the others with him.

REVEREND SYKES: Rev. Sykes is the black minister of the First Purchase Church, called that because it was paid for with the first money earned by the freed slaves. He's an imposing man with a strong stage presence. He should have a strong "minister's" voice.

HECK TATE: Heck is the town sheriff and a complex man. He does his duty as he sees it, and enforces the law without favor. The key to this man's actual feelings is revealed in his final speeches to Atticus, and this attitude should be an undercurrent to his earlier actions.

STEPHANIE CRAWFORD: She's a neighborhood gossip, and she enjoys it to the hilt. There's an enthusiasm in her talking over the people of her town that makes it almost humorous. Sometime she says things that are petty, but partly it's because she simply can't keep herself from stirring things up.

NATHAN RADLEY: He is a thin, leathery, laconic man. Note: This role may easily be doubled with that of Boo Radley. If so, Nathan should usually be seen wearing a hat, and when he appears as Boo, he should be wearing quite different clothes.

BOO RADLEY: Arthur Radley is a pale recluse who hasn't been outside his house in fifteen years. It takes an extraordinary emergency to bring him out, and once out he's uncertain about how to deal with people, and with his mission accomplished, he's eager to return to his sanctuary.

MRS. DUBOSE: She is an old woman -- ill, walking with difficulty, her pain making her biting, bitter, and angry. However, she's fighting a secret battle within herself, a battle about which few people are aware, and her existence has in it a point of importance for Jem and Scout.

TOM ROBINSON: Robinson is black, handsome and vital, but with a left hand crippled by a childhood accident and held against his chest. He's married to Helen and they have young children. He faces up to a false charge with quiet dignity. There's an undercurrent in him of kindness, sensitivity and consideration.

HELEN ROBINSON: She is half numb with the shock of the false charge against her husband Tom; she's someone caught in a nightmare.

JUDGE TAYLOR: The judge is a wintry man of the South, who does what he can within the context of his time to see justice done in his court. While he tries to run his court impartially, his sympathy is with Tom.

MR. GILMER: He is a public prosecutor who is doing his job in trying to convict Tom. In many ways his manner is cruel and hurtful. And yet under all this, he too has unexpressed doubts as to Tom's guilt, and his heart isn't really in this conviction. Still -- he goes after it, and it's a hard thing.

BOB EWELL: Ewell is a little bantom-cock of a man who lives with his large family by the town dump. As Harper Lee describes their situation -- "The town gave them Christmas baskets, welfare money, and the back of their hand." Bob thinks this trial will make him an important man, and when Atticus destroys his credibility, Bob's rage and frustration border on paranoia.

MAYELLA: The oldest daughter of Bob Ewell, she's a desperately lonely and overworked young woman whose need for companionship -- any companionship -- has overwhelmed every other emotion. However, when her effort to reach out explodes in her face, she fights just as desperately for what she thinks is survival.

To Kill a Mockingbird

NOTES ON COSTUMES

The time of the play is 1935 and the setting is a small town in a rural area of southern Alabama. The costumes should <u>suggest</u> this time and place; while there is no objection to the costumes being entirely authentic, this certainly isn't necessary. It should be remembered that this was the time of the great depression and there was very little money in towns like Maycomb, Alabama. The professional men such as Atticus, Judge Taylor and Mr. Gilmer wear business clothes, but they're old business clothes. Heck Tate and Nathan Radley wear a combination of business-work clothes. Such ladies as Maudie Atkinson and Stephanie Crawford wear quite nice clothes, but probably they've been kept nice by careful repair. Tom Robinson and Walter Cunningham wear neat, clean farm clothes -- but they should obviously be worn and used. Calpurnia dresses in impeccably neat work clothes, because that's the way she is. Mrs. Dubose is ill and even though she lives in a warm climate, she wants to be warmer, and she should have an old shawl. Helen Robinson's clothes are quiet, almost as though to foreshadow that she's about to become a widow. Mayella and her father wear clothes that have been given to them -- not absurd misfits, but at least suggesting that they're secondhand. Reverend Sykes wears a conservative dark suit, white shirt, and dark tie. Scout and Jem wear sensible play clothes -- at the beginning Scout wears bib-overalls. Dill is better dressed and more conscious of his appearance than the others. Jean Louise, however, stands out from the others because she belongs to <u>this</u> time rather than 1935. Her clothes should be quiet and unobtrusive, but definitely of the present. Boo Radley, being a recluse, wears shabby comfortable clothes.

PROPERTIES

GENERAL

<u>Street:</u> Porch fronts with railings, practical doors behind them; picket fence; tree; rockers, chairs, old-fashioned radio, porch swing or glider on Finch porch; potted flowers, chair draped with shawls on Dubose

porch; shutters and curtains at window of Radley house; flowers or
shrubs about houses (optional).

<u>Courtroom</u>: Judge's bench and chair, witness chair, small table and chair,
table with two chairs.

PERSONAL

SCOUT: Piece of gum and small box (supposedly taken from knothole in
tree); two soap carvings in pocket.

CALPURNIA: Dish cloth.

HECK TATE: Heavy rifle; slip of paper, flashlight.

JUDGE TAYLOR: Gavel.

MRS. DUBOSE: Cane.

JEM: Football; small flashlight.

ATTICUS: Eyeglasses, brief case, small folding chair, electrical extension
cord with light bulb on end, standing hat rack, newspaper, handkerchief;
envelope and fountain pen in pocket, papers.

MR. CUNNINGHAM: Sack.

SPECTATORS at Trial: Small folding chairs.

BOB EWELL: Piece of wood, knife.

MR. GILMER: Papers.

DIRECTOR'S NOTES

DIRECTOR'S NOTES

DIRECTOR'S NOTES

DIRECTOR'S NOTES